The look Amanda gave me was so intense, so searching, I almost couldn't hold her stare. "Because I trust you, Hal."

She waited a beat, completely comfortable with our staring at each other. Then, the second before I had to look away, she took my hand gently in hers. "I trust you completely, Hal."

"Well, thanks," I said. "I appreciate your trusting me, Valentino." I was half joking, half serious when I added, "But you should probably put me to the test, you know? See if I'm worthy."

Amanda took off her glasses, leaned her head back against the seat, and smiled what I had come to think of as her Mona Lisa smile. "Oh, I will, Hal Bennett. I will."

the AMANDA project

Revealed

BOOK TWO
BY AMANDA VALENTINO
AND PETER SILSBEE

HARPER TEEN

An Imprint of HarperCollinsPublishers

FOURTH STORY MEDIA
NEW YORK

HarperTeen is an imprint of HarperCollins Publishers.
Revealed
Text copyright © 2011 by Fourth Story Media
Illustrations copyright © 2011 by Fourth Story Media

Fourth
Story
Media

Fourth Story Media, 115 South Street, 4F, New York, NY 10038

www.epicreads.com

Library of Congress Cataloging-in-Publication Data
Valentino, Amanda.
    Revealed / by Amanda Valentino and Peter Silsbee. —1st ed.
        p.   cm. — (The Amanda project ; bk. 2)
    "Fourth Story Media"
    Summary: As high school freshmen Hal, Callie, and Nia try to
uncover why their enigmatic friend Amanda suddenly disappeared, they
learn that they and their families may be closely tied to the mystery.
    ISBN 978-0-06-174215-6
    [1. Mystery and detective stories.   2. Missing persons—Fiction.
3. High schools—Fiction.   4. Schools—Fiction.   5. Interpersonal rela-
tions—Fiction.   6. Family life—Maryland—Fiction.   7. Maryland—
Fiction.]   I. Silsbee, Peter.   II. Title.
PZ7.V2525Rev   2011   2010042673
[Fic]—dc22   CIP
                                                          AC

Book design by Polly Kanevsky and Dale Robbins
11 12 13 14 15   LP/BV   10 9 8 7 6 5 4 3 2 1
❖
First Edition

for cornelia and deirdre
    whose patience and impatience
    i hope are herewith rewarded

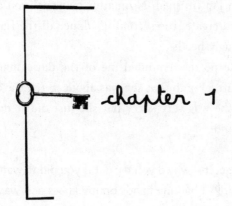

chapter 1

Vice Principal Thornhill's office didn't look like a crime scene. Of course, sitting in the outer office Monday morning and waiting to be questioned by the police, I could only see his door. Maybe inside everything was blood and broken glass and chalk outlines where his body had fallen after he'd been attacked sometime between six P.M. Friday (when his secretary, Mrs. Leong, the last person to speak to him, had said good night) and seven A.M. Saturday (when Mr. Richards had come in to ask him a question about football uniforms and found him lying on the floor of his office, unconscious and bleeding from a blow to the head).

The image of Thornhill lying there hemorrhaging made my stomach turn over, and I looked for something to distract me from whatever was behind his office door. My eyes wandered over to the poster I'd designed as a favor to my art teacher for the upcoming production of *As You Like It*, but as soon as they landed on it, I let them slide past—I never like looking at my artwork when I'm finished. No matter how cool you are with something you create, the second it's done, all the flaws start rearing their ugly heads.

Seeing the poster reminded me of the day Amanda had dropped her little bomb that she was about to tell the director, Ms. Garner, she was very sorry but she just didn't have time to play Rosalind.

"I don't get it—why'd you try out if you didn't want to take the part?" I had my hands on my knees and was sucking air. Super-macho, I know.

It was early morning, just the slightest dusting of color in the sky, and I'd been for a run in the crisp winter solitude. As I was passing the turnoff to Crab Apple Hill, I came upon Amanda—in the months that we'd been friends I'd gotten used to her showing up where I least expected her to, and now I was only moderately surprised to run into her (sometimes literally) in the strangest places (i.e., in the woods at the crack of dawn in the middle of winter).

She was leaning up against a tree wearing a pale green dress with an honest-to-god daisy chain in her hair. I had just enough time to wonder where she'd gotten daisies in February before she reached up and placed an identical ring of daisies on my head.

"Here. We can pretend they're laurels." She bit her lower lip and considered me for a long minute. "Though maybe daisies are acceptable given that you're an artist and not a poet."

"Or given that I'm neither," I corrected her. Amanda always insisted I was an artist—a great artist. Sometimes I accused her of getting me entered into that national art contest I'd won just so she could win our ongoing argument about whether I had any talent.

"'If you hear a voice within you say, "You cannot paint," then by all means paint, and that voice will be silenced.'"

It was impossible not to smile in the face of her confidence in me, but in our friendship we had a tradition of teasing each other, so I kept up my end of the banter. "Don't you try to impress me with your quotes, Amanda Valentino."

"Don't you try to convince me with your insecurities, Hal Bennett."

"*Touché.*"

"*Au contraire. Coulée.*"

I shook my head—we'd pretty much reached the limits of my French before *touché*. She smiled at me, her enormous gray-green eyes crinkling at the corners.

"You look like something out of Greek mythology in that." I gestured to show I meant more than the dress, that I was including the daisy chain and the sandled feet, even the tree she was leaning against.

"I love the Greek gods. Don't you?"

"Umm . . ." It wasn't that I *didn't* love the Greek gods, I'd just never really thought about it. Zeus. Poseidon. They were cool for sure. But could you *love* them?

Amanda continued, swinging her arms around as we walked. "They're so human. Those jealous rages. Those desperate disguises." Stopping, she placed her hands on the sides of her face. "Now you see them." She covered her eyes with her long, tapered fingers. "Now you don't."

"You'd better work on that disappearing act before you tell Ms. Garner you're not taking the part of Rosalind. She's going to lose it."

We started walking again, the slight crunch of our feet on fallen leaves the only sound in the early morning quiet.

Amanda inhaled the cold, misty air, held her breath for a second, then exhaled. She finally shivered in the cold. "Don't you think that's exactly the problem with the Ms. Garners of the world? They are *always* looking for an excuse to go crazy."

I knew what she meant. I hardly knew Ms. Garner—our only exchange had been when I'd shown her some preliminary sketches for the *As You Like It* posters. But even that brief conversation had given me the heebie-jeebies—the way she placed her hand on my arm and thanked me so intensely you'd think I'd donated a kidney. *Hal Bennett*, she'd said, *you are a lifesaver*. Her eyes had literally welled up, and I found myself patting her shoulder gently, like my sketches were a piece of bad news I had to help her through.

Still, Ms. Garner wasn't any more or less crazy than she'd been when Amanda had auditioned and turned the school upside down by winning a role Heidi Bragg (star of stage, screen—well, okay, just stage—and queen bee of the ninth grade at Endeavor High) had been guaranteed to land.

I stopped walking and turned to face her. "Why change your mind, Amanda? Why *not* star in the play?" The truth was I didn't give a rat's behind if Amanda starred in the play or told Ms. Garner to take the part of Rosalind and—well, I just didn't care.

What I cared about was the feeling I was starting to have, even then, that there was something impermanent about Amanda's being in Orion. In my life. When she'd auditioned for the play, I'd taken it as a promise that she'd be at Endeavor through opening night at least. Her dropping out even before rehearsals began made me afraid the play wasn't the only thing she would be leaving soon. That our friendship had an expiration date.

"Why not star in the play?" she repeated. Then she lifted her chin so we were looking into each other's eyes. "I fear theater just is not my art form of choice, Hal."

"What's your art form of choice, then?" I'd meant my question to be light, jokey, but it came out as serious as anything I'd ever asked her.

She kept her eyes locked on mine for another beat. "Life," she answered. She stepped back, away from me. "All the world's a stage, Hal!" A second later, she gathered up the long skirt of her dress and took off, the wood nymph I'd said she looked like. "Race you," she called over her shoulder.

And even though I was once the star sprinter on the Endeavor track team, she'd gotten enough of a head start that I couldn't catch her.

I shook my head, trying to clear Amanda from my thoughts. I needed to focus. I was about to be interrogated by the police, and given the über-questionable nature of my extra-curricular activities over the past couple of weeks, I'd better have my answers prepared.

It wasn't that there was *no* reason for me to be sitting here that made me so uneasy. It was that there were too many reasons. Like the fact that a week before Thornhill was found in his office, Callie Leary, Nia Rivera, and I had broken into his office while serving detention, looking for clues as to how he was so positive Amanda Valentino vandalized his car and framed us for it. Or how about our breaking into his car *after* he was found, when the three of us decided we absolutely had to know if Amanda had left him the note Callie and I thought we'd seen in his car. (She had.)

For the first time in my life, I understood why people said that something that was clearly really, really stupid in retrospect had seemed like a good idea at the time. Because what had felt logical—necessary even—just two days ago, seemed pretty dimwitted now that I was sitting and waiting to be questioned by the law.

Just as I was reassuring myself that the fact that I'd been called to the office alone meant nobody on the Orion police force knew about the extra-legal activities Nia and Callie and I had been doing, the door to the main office flew open and Callie stepped in. My heart sank; there was no denying that her arrival was a bad sign. Had we left fingerprints in the car? Traces of our break-in to Thornhill's office?

Only everywhere.

Still I couldn't *not* be happy to see Callie. She smiled at me and made her way over to the empty chair next to mine. As she crossed the office, she pushed her red hair back from her face, and I noticed it was curly again, like it had been the summer before sixth grade, when we'd been friends and hung out fishing and rock climbing and discovering secret caves in the woods. All that was back before she'd become an I-Girl— one of the coven of girls, led by Heidi, that ran the ninth grade. I wondered if her having curly hair instead of blown-out perfection had something to do with her *not* being friends with Heidi Bragg and company anymore or if it was just a temporary change. Either way, there was no denying how pretty Callie looked.

"Hey," I said as she slid into the seat next to mine.

"Hey," she said. Our voices were low even though Mrs. Leong wasn't sitting at her nearby desk giving us her usual evil eye.

Letting her bag slide to the floor, Callie asked, "This is probably a bad sign, isn't it?"

"What, you mean our having committed a couple of break-ins together and now being hauled in by the police?" I bent down and pretended to tie my shoe in case the other secretary who sat across the office was watching us. "Please," I whispered, my eyes on the shoelaces I had to untie to retie. "We're criminal masterminds. Look, they didn't even figure out Nia's with us."

"Um, yeah, about that . . ." When Callie didn't finish her sentence, I sat up and looked at her, and she gestured with her eyes at the office door. I turned to see what she was looking at and found myself staring at Nia through the window, her hand about to open the door. When she saw me and Callie, her eyes widened, but she came over to us without saying anything.

If Callie looked pretty, Nia looked . . . Nia looked like a

7

cutting-edge fashion model. She was wearing a short, tight black jacket that puffed out a little at the waist and these really rad cropped pants. The heels of her men's oxfords clicked on the linoleum floor as she crossed it. Her 1950s-style glasses set off her huge brown eyes. Like I said, I don't normally notice much about girls' wardrobes, but in the past few months, Nia had gone from super-baggy-jeans girl to super-hipster girl.

There was no way to *not* notice that.

Nia sat down next to Callie, crossed her legs, and mimed taking a drag on an invisible cigarette. Then, cool as a cucumber, she declared, "Well, fancy meeting you here."

The secretary across the room stood up and disappeared into a small alcove near her desk. A second later, we heard the sound of a fax machine being dialed.

"Um, is this the part where we get our stories straight?" asked Callie.

Nia arched her eyebrow. "Which story in particular? The one about why we broke into his car or the one about how we have a key to his office?"

I, for one, had forgotten about the key.

"You know," Callie continued, undaunted. "Like, where were you on Friday night between the hours of six P.M. and seven A.M.?"

"'Out searching for Amanda Valentino' probably isn't the alibi that's going to make us sound especially innocent," Nia answered.

"Or sane." I remembered our fruitless search for Amanda, how we'd traveled from one end of Orion to the other without finding anything except for evidence that we weren't the only people searching for her and a trail of clues she'd left for us that seemed to say simply: Keep looking.

Just then a door opened to our right and, as if they were strung together, we swung our heads in unison toward the sound. But it wasn't the door to Thornhill's office that had opened; it was the door *next* to his office door—a door I'd always just assumed led to a closet. As it swung shut, and Mrs. Leong exited, I got a glimpse of a table and a couple of chairs. I wondered if the room she'd been in had a door connecting it to Thornhill's office, and as I did, I was overwhelmed by a sudden thought so powerful it was almost a physical sensation:

I needed to get into Thornhill's office.

Every once in a while I get a feeling about something— a . . . well, a sense, I guess you could call it. And when I get that feeling, I'm never wrong. It's how I figured out that Amanda's graffiti on the car wasn't just graffiti, it was a message; how I knew the attack on Thornhill wasn't just a random irate parent, it was connected to Amanda.

I'm trying to avoid the word *psychic* here.

Mrs. Leong walked past us and out into the hallway, her face streaked with tears.

Should I tell Callie and Nia what I was thinking, ask them for help? Maybe it was better if they didn't know. Just as I decided to wait until one of the girls was pulled in for questioning, then dash into Thornhill's office without involving them at all, the fax-sending secretary came out of the alcove and crossed over to sit directly next to Thornhill's office door.

So much for Plan A.

As she picked up a ringing phone, I turned to face the girls, my voice low and urgent. "This might sound crazy, but I need to get into Thornhill's office."

Nia raised her eyebrows. "And it's déjà vu all over again."

"Hal . . ." Callie's face wrinkled with concern. "Don't you think—"

My eyes were back on the door to the little room, and as I watched, the knob began to turn from the inside. There wasn't much time.

"I can't explain it," I said quickly. "I just need a few minutes alone in there, okay? Can you create some kind of—" The door began to open.

"Henry Bennett?" An Orion cop who looked so much like a policeman it was as if he were auditioning for the pilot for *CSI: Orion* appeared in the open doorway. He was enormous, maybe six five or six six, his uniform crisp and tan, his hair clipped like he was about to ship out with the marines for points unknown.

At his hip was a holstered gun.

"Hal..." Callie repeated, and this time her voice was a plea.

"I know what I'm doing," I mumbled, barely moving my lips.

I stood up and slung my backpack over my shoulder, wondering if I'd ever uttered a bigger lie in my life. It had been terrifying enough to break into Thornhill's office when he was supervising detention in the library on the other side of the school. Was I really going to do it when an officer of the law— an officer of the law whose biceps literally strained the seams of his XXL uniform—was just on the other side of the door?

My throat was dry as I made my way past the policeman and toward the seat he indicated was for me. The windowless room wasn't much bigger than a closet; the square table with four chairs around it took up almost the entire space. But its Lilliputian dimensions didn't concern me any more than the stale smell of coffee that hovered over everything. All I cared about was the answer to my question, and it stood directly behind the chair I took.

A door.

A door that, given what I knew about the location of Thornhill's office, could only lead to one place.

"So—Henry Bennett."

"Hal," I corrected him. "Nobody calls me Henry." When I'm in trouble with one of my parents, I get called Henry, so what I'd just said wasn't entirely true. But I had the feeling I was going to be telling Officer . . . Nick Marciano (according to his name tag) many things that weren't entirely true in this interview.

"Hal," he repeated, but it was clear he couldn't have cared less what my name was. Leaning back in his chair, he crossed his arms in front of his chest and looked up at the ceiling, like he was reading a script off the fluorescent light that buzzed above us. "So . . . Hal." His voice was casual, almost friendly. "Why do you think I've called you in here? You and your friends Nia and Callie?"

"Um . . . you're lonely?" I offered.

In a nanosecond, laid-back-musing-at-the-ceiling Officer Marciano was replaced with scary-finger-in-Hal's-face Officer Marciano. "Don't get smart with me, Hal Bennett. A man was nearly killed in that room on Friday night." He pointed to the door behind me. "Someone smashed the security cameras, entered the building, and attacked the vice principal of the school. I want to know what you know about it."

"But, sir, why would I know anything about Mr. Thornhill's attack?" I asked. It was true. I may have known some things about Thornhill that I wasn't supposed to know. And I'd definitely *done* some things I wasn't supposed to have done. But I had no idea who'd attacked him or why.

"Yes, why indeed, Hal Bennett. Why would the three people who created 'The'"—he looked down again at the sheet in front of him—"'Amanda Project' know anything about a mysterious attack on Roger Thornhill."

I was so surprised I couldn't *not* react. "What!?"

I'd expected to be asked about breaking into Thornhill's car or maybe even the downloaded surveillance footage we took from his computer (could they tell that when they did forensics on his computer? Can they even *do* forensics at the Orion Police Department?) but what did The Amanda Project website have to do with the vice principal getting clobbered?

Officer Marciano was pleased by my surprise, you could tell. "Oh, now we're getting somewhere, aren't we?" His voice was both threatening and sickly sweet, a honey-dipped switchblade. "Yes, *Hal*"—there was something so creepy about the way he said my name that I wished, suddenly, I'd just let him go on calling me Henry—"you and your friends thought you could put one over on us, didn't you? You thought—"

"Oh my god, I can't *take it anymore!*" The voice that came from the outer office was high-pitched and hysterical, and I immediately recognized it as Callie's. For a second, I wanted to push Officer Marciano out of the way and run and comfort her, but just as my leg muscles tensed, I realized what was happening.

My diversion.

"You have to relax! It's going to be okay." Despite her calming words, Nia's voice sounded almost as hysterical as Callie's. "Callie, don't!"

"Girls! Girls!" the secretary cried.

Officer Marciano was on his feet and out the door in a split second. "What is going on out here, ladies?" The door closed automatically behind him.

All I heard was the first part of Nia's response, "Callie's completely—" before I, too, was on my feet and out the door.

Albeit a different one.

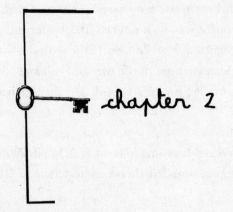

chapter 2

The lights were out in Thornhill's office, but there was an entire wall of windows that let in enough sun for me to see just fine. Contrary to my *CSI*-inspired fantasies, the room looked much the way it had when we'd broken into it a little over a week ago. There was no shattered glass, no overturned chairs. The only sign of the crime that had been committed was a dark spot on the rug in front of the desk that I told myself could just as easily be spilled coffee as blood (though it was hard to explain why the police would have put a square of yellow "Crime Scene: Do Not Cross" tape around a coffee splotch).

The need I'd had to get into the office had grown stronger as I crossed the threshold, but looking around me, I started to feel a little insane. What had I hoped to find, anyway? The police had probably been swarming the room all weekend—surely if there was any clue to be found, they'd already unearthed it.

The desk was as pristine as it had been the day he'd called me, Callie, and Nia in to ask us about the graffiti on his car and Amanda's disappearance—nothing on its surface but the blotter, a phone, a laptop, and a notepad with Endeavor Unified Middle and High School printed at the top. I flipped through the pages, but they were blank. Glancing over at an ancient computer on its stand, I saw an empty coffee cup and a plastic spoon in the metal garbage can beside it. Did they belong to the criminal? To Thornhill? To the police who'd searched the room looking for clues? Maybe I should take them. They were probably dripping with DNA samples.

Oh, yes, Hal, that's an excellent *idea. You can use your DNA-removal kit to separate the genetic material from the plastic and then run the results through your crime lab's computer.*

Not.

Okay, okay, the DNA thing was a little ridiculous.

A scream, the sound of something (a cell phone?) hitting linoleum. *"What if the person comes back? What if we're being targeted?!"* Despite my terror, I couldn't help smiling at Callie's performance and loving her for it. Amanda may have gotten cast as Rosalind in *As You Like It* and Heidi may have taken the role when Amanda turned it down, but clearly Callie was a girl with her own hidden talents.

Still, as good an actress as Callie was, how much longer could she hold Officer Marciano out there? Sooner or later—probably sooner—he'd calm her down or send her home.

I'd been in Thornhill's office for almost a minute and I'd discovered nothing.

As my eyes swept the desktop for a second time, the tiny glow of the laptop's power light caught my eye.

Wait a minute—since when did Thornhill have a laptop? Endeavor wasn't exactly on the cutting edge of the technological revolution—my little sister, Cornelia, who's basically a computer genius, had recently been home sick with strep, and my mother had called to ask her history teacher if Cornelia could scan and email him the homework she'd been doing while she was absent. His response had been, and I quote, *That is not what computers are for, Mrs. Bennett.*

Gotta love an institution with both feet firmly in the twentieth century.

Casually, as if someone was watching me and I had to make it look accidental, I made my way around the desk, then flipped open Thornhill's laptop, keeping the sleeve of my rugby shirt between my fingertips and the computer. Maybe *I* didn't know how to dust for fingerprints, but surely the Orion Police Department did.

The screen immediately hummed to life, a document opening up before my eyes. But it was just a memo to the teachers about a new system for getting classroom supplies for next year: . . . *will be available as of April and can be retrieved either by filing a request with Mrs. Leong in the main office or by* . . .

What was I doing? I probably had about ten seconds before Officer Marciano burst through the door with his gun drawn, and I was reading a memo about Post-its.

My T-shirt-covered finger couldn't move the arrow up to the task bar, so I used the edge of my pinkie to get there and click on FILE. Did the sides of your fingers leave prints? No doubt. My eyes raced down the list of files Thornhill had recently opened. *Cell phone policy changes; Letter of Rec. Dr. Thomas; Minutes, March Board Meeting; Cast list*—Much Ado About Nothing; *Spring events—tentative (no athletics); Spring events—definite (athletics).*

Well, what had I expected—*Thornhill's possible attackers (definite)*? I scanned the list one more time, the pointlessness of the whole enterprise overwhelming. There was nothing here. There was nothing anywhere. How many times had we checked the website for clues about Amanda's disappearance, only to discover everyone who knew her was as mystified (and misled) as we were?

Why should Thornhill's attack be any different?

I stood up and put my hand on the computer to shut it when my eyes caught the name of a file one last time.

Cast list—Much Ado About Nothing.

Much Ado About Nothing.

But *Much Ado About Nothing* wasn't the play being put on at Endeavor this year. The play being put on at Endeavor this year was *As You Like It*.

Could Thornhill have made a mistake? Or could he have the cast list from a *previous* year's play? For a second I tried to remember what play the high school had put on last year, and then I was sliding the arrow back up to the file menu and clicking open the cast list (misnamed or otherwise) for *Much Ado About Nothing*.

The document that opened before my eyes was nothing like any cast list I'd ever seen. It looked more like the files my dad sometimes brings home from his work as an accounting consultant, columns of data that made absolutely no sense—words that seemed to morph into numbers, numbers that stretched on forever. C-33528, F-514, M-229, beta file-4421(a). Dem_94. At first, I was so overwhelmed by the meaningless information that swam in front of me I could barely make sense of the rows and columns, much less the data they contained. And then the senseless mass began to make sense.

The font was tiny, so small I had to squint to read it, but the left-hand column of the chart was definitely a list of names in no particular order that I could discern. At first, they meant nothing. There was a *Reeve, Cecile* and *Hayes, Gracie*. But as my eyes slid down the column, they landed on a name that did mean something to me. In fact, it meant a great deal to me.

Because it was mine.

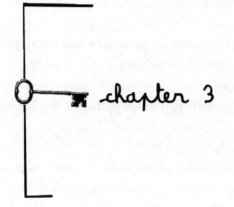

chapter 3

Bennett, Henry.
   Bennett, Cornelia.
   Bennett, Katharine.
   Bennett, Edmund.

Cornelia? What did my sister have to do with this? And my *parents*? What were my parents doing on Thornhill's list?

My heart began to pound so fast I almost couldn't breathe. There was Callie's name and Nia's, Callie's mom's and Nia's parents' names. I made my way down the list, my eyes moving too fast to read more than a few of the names I was racing through. Was Amanda's name there? I scrolled to the bottom, but there seemed to be no bottom, just hundreds and hundreds of names. I needed to write them all down. I needed to print out the list. I needed—

"For the last time, get a hold of yourself, Callista!"

Print. I needed to print. Hands shaking, I hit Apple, P, and as I did, the computer gave a strange sound, almost a sigh, and the screen went blank. A second later, the computer turned itself off.

"What?" Forgetting the need to be silent, forgetting everything except that I had to get that list, I hit the power key. Nothing happened.

"No," I whispered, frantically hitting the key again and again.

Nothing.

"*. . . so when I come back out, I want you gone. I want you on your way to the nurse. Do you understand me, young lady?*"

And as surely as I'd known I had to get into Thornhill's office, I knew now that I had to get out.

Officer Marciano opened the door to the conference room less than a second after I had literally jumped into my seat, the metal watch in my pocket digging into my leg hard enough to make me wince. Instead of taking my leg's being slung over one arm of the chair as an indication that I'd been on the move, he interpreted it as more evidence of my bad attitude.

Luckily, he didn't seem to notice that I was panting as hard as if I'd just run the fifty-yard dash—which, basically, I had.

"I'll thank you to sit respectably when you're in the presence of the law, young man," he said. Despite the bark in his voice, he looked a little less sure of himself than he had before he'd confronted Callie's hysteria. I remembered the time about a month ago when my mom had cooked this big dinner to welcome my dad back from a weeklong business trip. My mom's not exactly Martha Stewart, and she must have overcooked the roast, which we learned when smoke began pouring out of the oven and all the smoke detectors on the first floor started going off at once. She's usually pretty calm, but as soon as she realized the dinner she'd been planning and preparing for days had just caught on fire, she completely lost it.

Right about now, Officer Marciano looked kind of like my dad had on the way to the restaurant we went to that night, and when the cop's phone rang, he answered it with an enthusiasm that made me think he wanted nothing more than for it to be the news that some other violent crime had occurred and required his presence far, far from the world of hysterical high school girls.

"Marciano here," he barked. "Oh, hey, Jack . . . No, I'm talking to the Bennett kid now."

I tried not to visibly shudder. Why was Chief Jack Bragg, Heidi's father, asking about my interrogation?

"You sure? We only . . . right. Sorry, Jack. Will do." He snapped his phone shut and gave me a look of intense irritation. "We'll have to pick up this little conversation later."

I can't tell you how much I'm looking forward to it. "So, I'm free to go then?"

Officer Marciano gave me a long look. "You're free," he acknowledged. "But not to go. Not far anyway."

He stood up and so did I. But when he went over to the door, he just stood there. I looked at him, and he looked at me, and I realized he wanted me to know that he didn't have to open that door.

"Have a good day, *Henry*." Still he stood there, like he was just daring me to ask him to move.

What I needed was to get somewhere quiet, somewhere I could sit and try to remember the names that had been on that list. What I *didn't* need was to spend the rest of the afternoon trying to explain to my mother why I'd been arrested by the Orion police.

"Thank you. You too, sir." And with that, I slid around Officer Marciano and opened the door, slightly disappointed but not surprised to find that neither Callie nor Nia was waiting for me when I came out.

If there had been a quiz in either of my last two classes, I'd have failed it. For the ninety minutes between the end of my interview with Officer Marciano and the end of the school day, all I did was try and re-create the list I'd found on Thornhill's computer.

Callie, Nia, and I had definitely been on it. I was pretty sure there had been a Zoe on it, and the approaching end of the school day—with its promise of after-school munchies to feed my hunger—made me think of pasta, which made me think Zoe had an Italian last name . . . Costello? Wasn't there a Zoe in our grade? I was pretty sure there was, but I couldn't think of her last name.

Trying to remember even a dozen of the names on the list was giving me a colossal headache. Had Amanda's name been there? I'd been so sure I hadn't seen it. But could I have missed it? That seemed impossible—all I'd been doing lately was looking for clues as to where Amanda Valentino had disappeared. There was no way I could have missed seeing her name in black and white right in front of me. Still, there had been so many names. Could I have skipped it somehow?

And what was *my* name doing there? And my sister's? And my *parents'*? Mrs. Kimble wrote *beatitude* on the board and as I stared at the word it morphed and became something else. Bea. Beatrice. Had Beatrice Rossiter's name been on the list? Picturing her lying in a Johns Hopkins hospital bed and recovering from her plastic surgery, I wrote her name down, then crossed it out, then wrote it down again. While Mrs. Kimble droned on and on, I put my hands over my ears and hummed quietly to myself, trying to create a bubble of white noise to sound my memory.

When the bell rang at the end of the day, I literally sprinted to the door of the building, like Mr. Richards was standing there with his stopwatch. I needed to text Callie and Nia, to find out where they were and to tell them what I'd seen. I couldn't afford to get my phone confiscated, not now, so I made sure I had at least one foot out the door before I flipped open my cell. To my surprise, there was a text from Callie waiting for me.

CALL ME NOW.

I'd barely started dialing her number when there was a hand on my shoulder. I spun around and found myself looking into her green eyes, so wide it seemed there was nothing they couldn't see.

"I was just calling you." I held my phone out toward her as if to prove what I was saying.

"Nia's at Play It Again, Sam." Callie's voice was thick, like she was having trouble speaking. "She has bio last period and it was canceled and she got a text or something and she skipped last period and ran over there."

Play It Again, Sam was the vintage clothing store we'd gone to last week when we were looking for Amanda. I didn't mean to sound annoyed, but was this really the time for a shopping spree? "Nia went to buy *clothes*?"

"Hal, she found . . ." Callie swallowed hard, then pulled me over to the lawn, away from the throngs of people who were spilling out the front door into the freedom of afternoon. "She found everything there."

My brain was full of lists and names and numbers, and it was hard for me to focus on what Callie was saying. "She found what 'everything'?"

Callie put her hands on my shoulders, whether to steady me or herself, I wasn't sure. "Amanda's stuff. All of it. Her clothes, her costumes, her wigs—it's all there, at Play It Again, Sam."

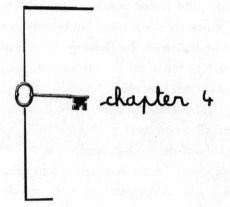 chapter 4

Callie and I didn't speak as we rode our bikes, single file, to Play It Again, Sam. We didn't need to. The look on her face made it clear that our thoughts were the same: There were only two reasons Amanda's stuff would have suddenly appeared somewhere without Amanda. One: She'd left Orion and was on the run. Two: She couldn't run anymore because she was . . .

I forced myself not to even consider the latter possibility. There was no way something terrible could have happened to Amanda without my knowing.

Oh, yeah? a voice in my head asked. *You'd "know"?*

Like how you "know" about the watch?

Thinking about the watch made me wince internally. The day Amanda disappeared, while I'd been washing her graffiti off Thornhill's car, she'd somehow gotten into my house and managed to hide an antique pocket watch in the leather jacket

I bought with her weeks before on our "independent field trip" (as she put it) to visit an artist she knew in Baltimore.

It was a beautiful pocket watch, really old school with black Roman numerals on a white background and works that had to be wound about five thousand times a day if you wanted the watch to run at all. On the back was an engraved message: *I know you (x2) know me.*

I know you (x2) know me.

I know you. x2. Know me.

What the *hell* was she talking about?

I'd spent practically every waking moment since I'd gotten the watch trying to decipher Amanda's message, but it was completely meaningless to me. She was trying to tell me something. Something she thought I'd understand. Something she needed me to understand. When I wasn't staring at the watch, I was holding it, eyes closed, practically chanting the mysterious words and numbers on the back. Maybe the x2 was meaningless, a red herring. Maybe the message was really straightforward—*I know you, Hal Bennett. You know me.*

You know me, too?

To you—know me!

Grr.

Amanda thought you could help her. She relied on you. But she was wrong, wasn't she? You don't know anything, do you, Hal?

I didn't have any feeling when I looked at the watch and its engraving. Didn't "know" she was telling me she knew me or I knew her. I tried to convince myself that was because the engraving probably wasn't even *from* Amanda—maybe she'd just gotten the watch for me because she liked it, because she knew I'd appreciate the beautiful spindly lines of the hands, the metronome-like tick of the seconds passing. She'd seen it in some thrift store and hadn't noticed (or had ignored) the message on the back, a message that some weird, alternative poet had written for her fiancé fifty years ago and that I was now misreading as a message from my friend.

Sure, Hal, sure. Running (possibly for her life), Amanda took the time to break into your house to drop off a gift with an engraved message you were meant to ignore. Like Hallmark, she simply cared to send the very best.

My daydreaming had caused me to fall behind Callie. I'm no Lance Armstrong, and as I pushed hard against the pedals in an attempt to catch up to her, I was glad for the ache the exertion caused in my calves. It helped dim the thought running like a chorus through my brain:

If I couldn't understand a straightforward message Amanda had left for me, how could I believe I'd know for sure if something really bad had happened to her?

We made a couple of wrong turns on the way to Play It Again, Sam, and when we finally leaned our bikes against the brightly painted porch and sprinted up the steps, it was getting dark. I knew I only had a little while before I had to be home—the school had sent out an email after Thornhill's attack saying all nonessential after-school activities were canceled pending further announcement. I'd noticed Endeavor's idea of essential (play rehearsal, basketball practice) and my idea of essential (time alone in the art studio, long-distance runs) proved just how different my priorities were from my school's, but Mom hadn't been interested in that point yesterday, and there was no reason to think she'd find it compelling now.

If I weren't home soon, there'd be hell to pay.

Last time we'd been here, I vaguely remembered the door had stuck and I'd had to push really hard against it, but Callie nudged it open easily, and the tiny bell above it tinkled into the silence of the seemingly empty room.

A disembodied voice called from the back, "Sorry, we're closed for inventory," and I recognized it as belonging to the owner, Louise. She'd told us she was closed for inventory Friday, too, and as I looked at the tons of clothes, scarves, earrings, shoes, boas, hats, and bags stacked on and hanging from every available surface, I realized the only surprising thing wasn't that she was closed for inventory but that she wasn't closed *down* for it.

"Hello?" Callie called.

"Callie? Hal?" It was Nia, her voice muffled by the vast quantities of stuff in the store.

"It's us," Callie responded.

Louise emerged from behind a mannequin, wearing a big faux-fur vest and vintage bell-bottoms, like some kind of urban hippie, her skin so black she could have been carved from a block of onyx. I'd forgotten how tall she was—I'm almost six feet, and she towered above me, her bright pink platform shoes no doubt adding a couple of inches to her height, but still. Her tank top revealed arms that could have given Officer

Marciano's a run for his money, and I made a mental note never to piss off Louise.

"Well," Louise said when she saw us, crossing her arms over her chest and looking us up and down.

"Hi," Callie said.

"Hi," I echoed lamely.

"I'm in the back," Nia called out.

Louise didn't indicate that it was okay for us to move farther into the store, but she didn't try to stop us, either. Callie took a hesitant step forward and I did the same, and then we were snaking our way through caverns of precariously piled boxes as we headed in the direction of Nia's voice.

At the back, the space opened up a little and there, sitting on the floor next to a coatrack, was Nia, holding a pair of sparkly red shoes. She looked up at us, her face tight with sadness and fear.

"It's all here. All her stuff."

Callie and I looked at the rack of coats, dresses, suits, and shawls packed together so tightly it was hard to see where one item of clothing ended and another began. The top was piled high with hats and wigs.

"My god," Callie whispered. She stepped forward and touched the sleeve of a black jacket so gently it was as if she thought it might be a mirage.

I cleared my throat. There was a pale green dress at the end of the rack closest to me that looked a lot like the one Amanda had worn that morning when she'd met me in the woods. "Um, are you . . . I mean, I know you know more about this kind of thing than I do, but are you guys sure this is her stuff?" It wasn't that the dress *wasn't* the one Amanda had been wearing that day, but that didn't mean it *was*.

Maybe emboldened by the fact that the sleeve hadn't dissolved into thin air when she touched it, Callie reached more surely into the rack, pulling out a plain gray dress. As soon as she saw it, Nia gasped. Callie turned to me, holding the dress against her.

"Even you must recognize this one, Hal. It's what she wore her first day of school."

"Hal Bennett, Amanda Valentino. Amanda Valentino, Hal Bennett."

It was the end of English class; Mrs. Kimble gestured from me to Amanda and back again, and Amanda extended her hand in my direction. I wasn't used to shaking hands with people who weren't friends of my parents, but I took hers. Her handshake was firm and confident, and I found myself hoping mine was, too.

"How do you do?" asked Amanda.

"Um, I do fine?" I'd meant to be funny, but I realized too late that my answer made me sound like either a loser or an ass.

Or, conveniently, both.

"How do *you* do?" I asked quickly.

My question was a throwaway line, but Amanda paused, seeming to consider it. "I'd have to say sunny, but with a chance of showers."

Mrs. Kimble giggled nervously. Under the best of circumstances she was hardly an island of calm, but Amanda's arrival had made her even more fidgety than usual. After Amanda pointed out that a quote Mrs. Kimble attributed to F. Scott Fitzgerald was actually something Ernest Hemingway had said *about* Fitzgerald, Mrs. Kimble never recovered. Twice she'd confused literal and figurative, and each time she vaguely maniacally laughed. I had the feeling she was running the words *leave of absence* through her otherwise empty head.

"Well, Amelia . . ."

"Amanda," Amanda corrected her.

Giggle. "Didn't I say that?" Giggle. There was a long pause as Mrs. Kimble's gaze darted nervously from Amanda to the hallway.

Her anxiety was contagious, so I wanted to flee the area quickly. "You wanted me for something?" I prompted her.

"Oh, yes, of course." She'd been focused on Amanda, a confused look on her face, but now she turned to me and her expression grew more sure. "Yes, I was going to ask that you escort"— she paused before speaking the name, afraid to get it incorrect again—"Amanda to her next class."

"Sure," I said. I turned to look at Amanda. She reminded me somehow of a painting, maybe a van Eyck or a Michelangelo. It wasn't that she was beautiful, exactly (though I guess she was), it was more that she was . . . timeless, like the *Mona Lisa* or Botticelli's *The Birth of Venus*. I felt both that I'd seen her face before—that I recognized it—and also that there was no one like her in the entire universe.

I realized I'd been staring, and I got embarrassed, but Amanda seemed not to mind. Or maybe not to notice.

Mrs. Kimble, on the other hand, appeared ready to pass out from anxiety. "Very well!" she screeched, and she gave a nervous clap of her hands. "Well, that's settled. And I'm sure you'll find Hal makes a *lovely* guide."

And suddenly I wasn't the only one who was staring. Amanda looked at me so intensely I had the sensation I'd never been looked at before.

Or maybe it was that I'd never been *seen* before.

It couldn't have been more than a moment that passed, but somehow it seemed we'd been standing there forever.

"Yes," she said finally. "I'm sure he *will* make a lovely guide."

Callie was shaking her head in mock despair. "Hal, you can't seriously tell me you don't remember her wearing this dress."

The moment, the meeting—it was all burned into my memory. But whether she'd been wearing a pair of jeans or a ball gown, no way could I have said.

I shook my head. "Sorry," I admitted. "I'm drawing a blank."

"Hal," Callie sighed. "Sometimes you're such a guy."

"You say that like it's a bad thing," I said, mock defensively.

"No," Callie said quickly. "I just meant . . . I just meant, yes, I'm sure it's the same dress." Our eyes met for a second and then she looked away and brushed something off her shoulder. The red of her hair shone against the dress she was holding, and I made a mental note to someday paint her wearing a gray dress.

"Hal, Callie." Nia's voice was a whisper, and when we

looked her way, she gestured for us to come closer. We went over to where she was sitting and kneeled beside her. "Louise texted me. She said she had Amanda's stuff. But when I got here, she wouldn't tell me how she got it."

As if drawn over by our discussion of her, Louise suddenly appeared between two towers of boxes. "So, you found it."

Nia stood up, still holding the sparkly red shoes. "You knew we would. That's why you texted me to come."

Louise shrugged. "Oh, I texted you?"

"You know you did. How did you get my number?" Nia folded her arms across her chest in a position I'd come to recognize as her don't-try-and-put-one-over-on-me-mister stance.

"Maybe a little bird gave it to—" Louise broke off; the sound of a car pulling into the empty parking lot her customers used made us all turn our heads toward the door.

"Why are you—" Nia began, but Louise put a hand up to silence her. I don't know if it was Louise's impressive bicep or her own confusion, but Nia shut her mouth. A moment later, we heard the car pull away.

"Lotta strange people been coming by here lately," Louise said, either to explain her response to the car in the parking lot or as an answer to Nia's question about why she'd contacted her.

But subtlety wasn't exactly Nia Rivera's middle name. "And how, exactly, did you get Amanda's stuff?" she demanded.

Louise looked down the length of the coatrack. "Is this hers?" she asked.

"What are you *talking about*?" Nia demanded. Callie put her hand on Nia's arm, but Nia turned to her and angrily shook it off. "She *texted* me!" she snapped at Callie. "And now she's acting like I'm crazy or something."

Louise ran her hand over her nearly shaven head and looked at Nia like she wouldn't have minded eating her for lunch.

Before Nia could say anything else, I stepped between the two of them. "Do you mind if we look through this stuff? I mean, will we interrupt your inventory?"

Louise turned her head slowly and squinted toward me. I realized I was holding my breath as I waited for her to decide.

When she walked away, I felt my heart sinking with a sense of having failed, but then, without turning around, she said, "Speaking of inventory, I wonder what's in all those pockets." And then, she disappeared from view.

Nia was fuming. "That woman is so totally—"

Callie still had her hand on Nia's arm, but it didn't look like they were about to come to blows anymore. "Look, obviously she doesn't want to tell us anything directly," Callie said quietly. "But she has Amanda's stuff and, like you said, she *did* contact us. So she *is* telling us something."

"What do people have against just communicating things *directly* lately?" Nia asked from between gritted teeth, and without her saying it, we all knew she wasn't just talking about Louise.

I'd never realized how many places girls have pockets. Amanda's skirts had side pockets and front pockets, decorative pockets that didn't open, decorative pockets that did. Some of the pockets had pockets, and at one point I put my hand in the pocket of a blazer and pulled out a small purse that was attached to the lining of the blazer by a long string.

Inside the purse was a pocket.

I don't know what we expected to find in the pockets, exactly, but the more mundane pocket-y things we pulled out of them, the more depressed we got. Here and there—between the pennies and the forgotten vocabulary sheets, the gum wrappers, and the used-up ChapSticks—we found the occasional thing that could only have come out of a pocket that Amanda had owned. A delicate handkerchief with a border of flowers embroidered into the shape of a graceful A; a quill with a thick blue feather atop it; a small book with pieces of paper that Callie and Nia explained were covered in something called dusting powder.

"It's so you can powder your nose," Callie said. Laughing, she ripped a piece out and touched it gently to the tip of Nia's nose. "There. Much better."

"Oh thank god—I was feeling soooo shiny."

Callie ripped off a second sheet and reached toward me. The paper felt smooth against my skin, and I closed my eyes slightly at the gentle pressure of Callie's fingers.

"Hey!" Nia's voice was excited, and Callie and I looked to see what earned a "hey" from unflappable Nia. She was pulling something out of the pocket of a hot pink raincoat.

"Movie tickets," I said, recognizing the familiar shape. I read the name and address of the theater off them. "They're from Los Angeles." I looked from Nia to Callie. "Did you guys

35

know she'd lived in Los Angeles?"

They both shook their heads as Callie read the title off the ticket in Nia's hand. "The Rudolph Valentino Film Festival." She looked up, startled and pleased. "Rudolph Valentino. Amanda Valentino. I wonder if that's a relative of hers. Maybe we can track him down."

Nia snorted. "Tell me you're joking."

Callie shook her head, bewildered at Nia's mocking her.

Still wearing her familiar expression of total disdain, Nia continued. "Did you, like, take a course in cultural illiteracy?"

I was starting to get a bad feeling about this conversation. "Um, guys, I think—"

Callie waved her hand in a way that indicated she wasn't interested in my playing sheriff at this showdown. "Don't start with me, okay, Nia? Whatever 'crime' you feel I've committed, just give me a break."

But either because she was still angry at Louise or Amanda, or because she was just such a big Rudolph Valentino fan that she couldn't bear the idea that someone somewhere in the world didn't know who he was, Nia wasn't about to let Callie's comment go. "You'll be happy to know, Callie, that we actually *could* track him down. In the *cemetery* where he's been *buried* for the past eighty years."

There was a pause and I thought for sure Callie was going to lay into Nia. Instead, she cocked her head to the side, like she was considering something. "So you're saying he's probably not, like, her dad, aren't you?"

I don't know if it was the averted fight or the tension of the whole day, but suddenly the three of us just cracked up. We laughed so hard I literally fell down, which made Callie and Nia pretty much completely hysterical. Every time I tried to get up, one of them would say the words "Rudolph Valentino" and we'd all start howling all over again. Finally I just gave up trying to get off the floor.

Eventually Nia took off her glasses, rubbed the bridge of her nose, and said, "Okay, guys, we have to focus here."

"Yes." Callie gave a final giggle and looked at the tickets one last time. Then she shrugged. "Rudolph Valentino. Amando Valentino. Well, Valentino's a good name anyway."

"Yeah, too bad he wasn't born with it. His real name was . . ." She squinted with the effort of recalling it, then snapped her fingers. "Rodolfo Alfonso Raffaello Piero Filiberto Guglielmi."

"That's a name?" Callie shook her head. "Sounds more like a class list from a school in Milan."

Nia nodded her agreement and went to put the tickets in our "Amanda" pile (as opposed to our "gum-wrapper-loose-change-and-random-homework" pile). "You can see why he made up Valentino."

And suddenly it hit me so hard I almost toppled over from my kneeling position. Callie must have noticed me catch myself. "Hal? What's up?"

At the sound of Callie's voice, Nia looked over at me, too.

I looked at both of them without seeing either. "So did Amanda."

"What?" they asked together.

I waited a minute, but the feeling didn't go away. "So did Amanda," I repeated. And in answer to their increasingly bewildered stares, I explained myself. "She made it up, too. Her last name? It isn't Valentino."

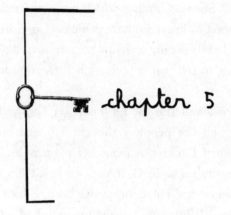
chapter 5

"What are you talking about?" Nia demanded.

"Look," I said, and I was about to explain how it's no big deal but sometimes I just, you know, "see things," ha ha, nothing strange about that, is there? When I realized I hadn't told them about the list I'd seen in Thornhill's office.

Kind of a big omission.

I took a deep breath. "Look, you're just going to have to believe me about her name and put it aside for a second because I have to tell you about something else right now and I need you to pay attention and not be distracted by whether or not I'm crazy."

"Oh, Hal." Nia put her hand on my shoulder in a mock comforting way. Her voice was pseudo-assuring. "We'd never say you're crazy." She paused, as if considering something. "Not to your face, anyway."

"And even if you are crazy," Callie assured me, "that doesn't mean we can't still be friends. We can *totally* visit you in the asylum." She was smiling, which made me smile, too.

"Always good to know I'll have company on visitor's day." I slapped my hands on my jeans to prepare myself. "Because what I'm about to tell you is pretty much the weirdest thing I've ever seen."

I explained about the list I'd found on Thornhill's computer, naming all the people I thought I'd seen on it. Nia looked pale when I told her about her parents, and Callie's mouth opened into a wide O at the news that her mother's name had been on it. "There must have been, I don't know, a hundred names," I finished. "Maybe two hundred." Thinking of the difference between how many names I'd seen and how few I actually remembered made me sick.

"And you're sure Amanda's name wasn't there?" Nia asked.

I shook my head and corrected her. "I'm sure I didn't *see* her name on it." I put my thumb and index finger a centimeter apart and held my hand in front of my face. "The font was this big. Plus, I'm pretty sure there were other pages I didn't get a chance to look at. Maybe I even saw it, only I didn't recognize it because I still thought Amanda *Valentino* was her real name."

Callie and Nia looked at each other, and Nia must have asked Callie a silent question because Callie just shrugged and shook her head.

Was this how people acted right before they call the men in little white coats to come and take you away?

I opened my mouth to defend my sanity, but before I could say anything, someone else spoke.

"You kids find the box?" I turned around. Behind me, Louise was standing on a ladder fishing what looked like a thousand pieces of yarn out of a white plastic bag jammed onto a shelf. She shook the yarn out in front of her and it revealed itself to be a vest.

"Cool," Nia observed.

"1965," Louise said, her appreciation for Nia's appreciation evident in her voice.

"Um, did you say something about a box?" Nia asked, and I wondered if she'd really liked the yarn-vest or if she'd been buttering up Louise.

"I might have," Louise acknowledged. "And if I were you, I'd likely look for it over there." She gestured just beyond the coatrack, which might have been helpful if the small area that she'd pointed to hadn't been crammed with about a thousand items piled together.

Nia headed toward it, pausing at an old-fashioned vanity table to lift a beautiful silver mirror from it. As she did, her face took on such a strange expression that I asked if she was okay.

"What?" She shook her head, almost as if she were emerging from a dream.

"I said, are you okay?"

"I just . . ." Her voice was soft and thoughtful. Extremely un-Nia. "There's so much sadness in this gift." She was still staring off into the distance, the mirror pressed to her chest.

Callie came up to Nia from around the other side of the coatrack. "What's that?" She reached for the mirror and took it from Nia, examining it closely. As soon as the mirror was out of her hand, Nia's face lost its dreamy look and went back to its more familiar semi-scowl.

"'To my dearest Fran on our wedding day—I will love you forever. George. October 4, 1917.'" Callie looked up, confused. "That's not sad, it's happy."

Nia rolled her eyes, then turned away from us and pushed her way deeper in the direction Louise had indicated we were to go. "Whatever," she mumbled.

"Why did you say it was sad?" I asked, following her.

I expected some acknowledgment of what I'd asked (maybe just an anti-romantic Nia crack), but even though we were only separated by a few feet, Nia seemed not to have heard me. Just as I was about to repeat my question, she gave a shout of discovery and pointed. On its side, wedged between an old phonograph and a marble-topped dresser table, was a box.

From the way Nia struggled to lift it, I could see it was heavy—I was about to offer to help when she said, without turning around, "Don't even offer, Hal Bennett. Yes, it's heavy. Yes, I can handle it."

"Oh. Well, great then." I stepped back as she gently shifted it forward and back several times, finally freeing it from where it had been trapped, getting it up on a corner and lifting it onto the vanity table.

"Wow," Callie said, reaching out a finger to stroke the ink-black wood.

"Very wow," Nia agreed.

"Seriously wow," I offered, ever helpful.

At first glance, the box seemed to be fine-grained black wood decorated here and there with turquoise, sometimes set directly into the wood, sometimes set into elaborate sunbursts of silver or mother-of-pearl. To my eye it looked slightly Native American, but that might have just been the turquoise. I stepped toward the box and went to open it, and it was only as I felt around for a lid or drawer that I realized there wasn't one.

"Um, Louise," Callie called.

As if she'd been hovering, waiting for us to call on her for help, Louise's reflection appeared in the mirror above the vanity. She looked at us looking at the box.

"Did you say . . . I mean, is this a *box* box?" Callie asked.

"You mean as opposed to what? A shoe box?" Her question wasn't exactly friendly, but the tone was gentle, teasing. I got the sense she was relieved that we were standing together around the box.

"She means does it open?" asked Nia. Her voice was pleasant, for Nia, but just as she finished asking, her phone buzzed angrily, like it was going to express the irritation Nia was holding in check. Nia looked to see who was calling, then blanched slightly. "Hi, Mama," she said, flipping it open. She stepped away from us quickly, but I could still hear her mom's angry flood of Spanish if not her exact words.

"Sorry," Nia said, her voice truly contrite. "I lost track of time."

Uh oh. I slipped my phone out of my pocket and saw I'd

43

missed three calls. It was late enough that I didn't have to wonder who'd called me.

My ass was grass.

Maybe because her dad's not exactly in the running for concerned parent of the year, Callie was the only one of the three of us who didn't seem panicked by the fact that we weren't home yet. Instead of clutching anxiously at her phone like it was about to ground her of its own volition, Callie had her face inches away from the box, which she was studying intently.

"Hal, look at this."

I moved over to where she was standing and got close to the box, like she was. And suddenly I saw why she'd been so amazed.

The wood wasn't fine-grained, as I'd thought at first. There was no grain at all. Instead, what I'd assumed was the pattern of a grain was actually a pattern cut into wood. The pattern was wild and more intricate than anything I'd ever seen. It looked like leaves and vines with creatures on them, but in the dim light of the store I couldn't make out exactly what I was seeing.

"It's beautiful," Callie whispered. She stood up and put her hands on the box, looking off into the near distance as she felt around the wood. "I can't find a way to open it, though."

Nia came back to where we were standing, snapping her phone shut in irritation. "Okay, I'm toast. My mom just gave me three minutes to get home, meaning I have about ninety seconds to develop the ability to fly."

"I think I'd better go, too," I said. My eyes were still on the box. Were we really supposed to just . . . leave it?

Like she'd read my mind, Louise observed, "Seems like you all could use a little more time with that box."

Callie was pretty much always nice, but now she turned on some serious charm. She flashed Louise her girl-next-door smile and (I am not kidding you here) actually folded her hands in front of her chest as if she were begging. "Um, Louise, I have a huge favor to ask you."

Like she knew exactly what Callie was doing, Louise released a burst of laughter. "Honey, save that sweet-girl show for your boyfriends." Callie blushed, but she didn't get pissed the way Nia might have.

"You're going to let us have the box, aren't you?" Nia's question wasn't an attack, it was a realization, and I understood that something had somehow been settled between them.

Louise didn't answer her directly. "That box needs to stay in the right hands," was what she said instead. "I hope you understand my meaning when I say it would be very, very dangerous for the wrong people to get ahold of it."

"We'll protect it," Callie assured her.

"We'll guard it with our lives," I added, because what might have sounded melodramatic a couple of weeks ago seemed called-for now.

Looking from one of us to the other, Louise slowly rubbed her hands together, almost like she was washing them. Then she nodded. "I believe you will." With that, she turned and walked even deeper into the back of the store. A minute later, we heard a door open and close.

The three of us looked at one another.

"We still don't know if it opens or not," Nia pointed out.

Callie took a step toward the table and picked up the box. The way it had been wedged between the furniture must have made it seem heavy because Callie didn't have to strain to lift it at all. Holding it extended in front of her, she looked down at the surface of the wood that seemed to ripple in the soft light.

And then, with Nia and me watching, she gently shook the box.

From inside, we heard the sound of something sliding back and forth.

"Well," said Nia into the silence of our amazement. "I guess we have our answer."

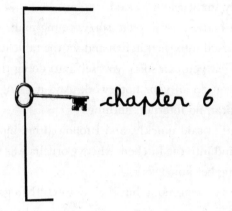 chapter 6

My mom was standing in the front hallway with her hands on her hips when I opened the door. One look at her face, and it wasn't hard to imagine she'd been in that exact position for the past several hours.

"Henry Bennett!" she announced the second she saw me, and I wondered why I'd been so scared of Officer Marciano. He had nothing on my mom.

"Do you realize that a man was *attacked* in his own office at your school? Do you know what it feels like when I'm driving home from work and I call your cell phone *three* times and get *no* answer? And then I call your sister and she says you haven't come home yet? Do you realize I am thinking you could be *dead* somewhere?" Her eyes welled up at her last question, but I knew now was definitely *not* the time to point out that obviously I wasn't dead, what with my having just walked in the front door.

"I'm really sorry, Mom," I said.

"Oh, you better *believe* you're sorry, young man. And you can sorry yourself into the kitchen and set the table for dinner and after we eat you can sorry yourself into doing the dishes right before you do all your homework. And nothing else, no games, no guitar, no internet, nothing."

"I'm on it!" I said quickly, and I followed my mom down the hallway and into the kitchen, where Cornelia was sitting at the table doing her homework.

My mom's a great mom, but she's not exactly a great cook (let's just say the burned roast wasn't character-illogical)—last year, when we re-did our kitchen, she jokingly asked the contractor if instead of a stove we could just get a phone with all the local take-out restaurants on speed dial. I saw a menu from John's Pizzeria open on the counter and had the feeling the doorbell would be ringing shortly.

As I set the table, my mom opened a bag of salad and tossed in some olive oil and vinegar, muttering something about "band practice" and being "too big a star to call your own mother." I realized she thought I'd been out with these sophomores who'd approached me a couple of weeks ago about playing with them in the upcoming talent show. At the idea that I'd spent my afternoon hanging out and playing Dylan riffs on my guitar, I didn't know whether to laugh or cry. If only my life were that . . . normal.

I grabbed some silverware from the drawer and put my

arms around my mom, kissing her on the cheek. "Mom, I promise. No matter how big a star I become, I'll never forget about you." I gave her a hug and she let me do it, which meant she was almost over being mad.

"You should feel free to forget about me," Cornelia said without looking up from her notebook.

"Who are you again?" I asked.

"Hardy har har." Cornelia tightened her ponytail, still studying the book in front of her.

People say my mom, Cornelia, and I look alike, probably because we all have blue eyes and pale skin. If you ask me, I'm not nearly as good-looking as the two of them—you're not supposed to say things like this about your mom, but when she was younger she was a total betty, as Amanda would have said (I've seen the photos). When Cornelia was a baby, people would literally stop on the street to say how pretty she was, and even though she's too young to be a hottie or anything, all signs point to her being gorgeous when she's older—not that I'd ever tell *her* that. She's already taller than a lot of the girls in her grade and her hair is the same excellent red as my mom's.

I've never really cared much about how I look, but this summer my mom's friend from her junior year abroad in France came to visit with her husband and daughter, Charlotte, who's sixteen. Charlotte was cool and everything, but she made a whole big deal about how I had to dress better and change my hair because (and I quote), "Hal, you are *dee-licious*." It was way embarrassing, but I let her take me shopping for new clothes, and we went to this salon in town where she told the woman how to cut my hair, which, apparently, was not delicious so much as it was a *"dee-sastaire!"*

Sitting in the salon covered in gunky hair gel while a woman wearing spandex demonstrated how I was supposed to *"shake* the shape into it, just *shake* the shape into it," I thought about all the great artists I admire. Picasso. Rembrandt. Giotto. The hairstylist said I should seriously consider getting something called lowlights (the opposite, apparently, of highlights).

It was hard to picture Michelangelo getting lowlights.

"I'm telling you, a *lot* of my customers are getting them these days." She fussed with my hair, pulling it against my cheek. "It would *really* bring out this gorgeous skin tone."

I told her I'd think about it just to get Charlotte to let me leave the salon. Then I was so pissed off I marched into a jewelry store right across the street from the salon and got my ear pierced. I don't know why exactly—I just felt like after a day spent with other people telling me what to buy and what to wear and how to shake my head I needed to make a decision for myself. The truth is, it hurt like hell, and my mom practically had a stroke when she saw what I'd done. I'm glad I did it, though. Partly because I kind of like how the little gold hoop looks, but mostly because it reminds me of a time I decided to do something and did it.

After dinner, the phone rang, but neither Cornelia nor I went for it. Sure enough, it was for my mom—some friend who wanted to know if my mom was free for lunch Friday. Within half a second, it was clear they were going to be on the phone for the next twenty minutes, which is a short conversation for my mother.

Cornelia and I may *look* like our mom, but sometimes I worry that in every other way, we resemble our dad. My mom is someone who's totally engaged in the world at all times. When I was a kid, she worked full-time *and* she was president of the PTA *and* she did all this volunteer community organizing *and* she found the time to help me and Cornelia do things like make dioramas for *The Lion, the Witch and the Wardrobe*. In between doing all of that, she had literally dozens of friends—work friends, college friends, friends who were the moms and dads of kids we went to school with, friends from her book group.

I remember my parents having all these conversations before we moved to Orion about whether my mom would be isolated if we came here, which in retrospect was nothing short of hilarious. We moved to Orion because of my dad's work (also hilarious—he travels so much it's hard to see how he actually works *here*), but within about a week (okay, maybe I'm exaggerating, but you get the idea) my mom had a big job in the admissions office at the local college and before you knew it, the phone was ringing a thousand times a second with her friends inviting her and my dad to people's houses for dinner every weekend and it was like we'd lived in Orion for years, not months.

But even though they have all these friends and they're constantly doing things with other couples, if you ever looked around the living room at one of their dinner parties, you'd notice that everyone present was there because one person in the couple is friends with my mom, not my dad. In fact, my dad doesn't really seem to *have* any friends—not even old friends from college or high school who he loves but only sees every few years. When people are over, he's usually somewhere just on the outside of things. Not in any crazy way—he's not, you know, standing in the corner staring at a wall. He's just . . . on the edge. Alone, even in a crowd.

I'd always thought he was just shy, but now I found myself wondering if there was more to the story than his personality.

Why were we on the list?

x0x0callicatx0x0: This box is incredible.

When we left Play It Again, Sam, we'd had to decide who was going to take the box. I said it probably wasn't a good idea for me to have it at my house. My mom's not a snoop, exactly, but she's in and out of my room, drawers, and closet with clean laundry and sheets and stuff just enough that I wouldn't want to promise she wouldn't find something I'd hidden and start demanding to know where I'd gotten it.

According to Nia, her mother *is* a snoop. So we gave the box to Callie because even though her dad's trying to stay sober and provide for them and stuff now, he's still a little more . . . distracted than Nia's and my parents.

artislifeisart94: can u describe it? i cant tell much from the picture u emailed.
NAR1010: yeah the flash kinda makes everything look washed out.

xOxOcallicatxOxO: theres a pattern, for sure.
& these little buttons or something.
NAR1010: you try pushing them?
xOxOcallicatxOxO: ya think?

Nobody typed anything for a minute, and I stared at the photo, trying to make out the buttons Callie had described. When my phone rang, I was still staring at the washed-out picture on my screen.

It was Callie. "I've got Nia on the line, too. We think we should post a picture of the box on the website."

"I don't know." I thought about Louise's warning. "What if the people who Louise is trying to keep the box from are monitoring the site?"

"What if they are? What are they going to do, break into one of our houses and steal the box?" Nia laughed at the preposterousness of her own suggestion.

Callie's voice was less amused. "Nia, these people may have attacked Thornhill in his office. Do you seriously think they'd hesitate to break into one of our houses?"

I'd learned enough in the time I'd known her not to push Nia when she was thinking about something. And sure enough, after a brief pause, she said, "Okay, you've got a point."

There was the squeak of my door opening and I spun around in my chair; obviously our discussion of break-ins was giving me the heebie-jeebies.

But it was just Cornelia, carrying a bowl of chocolate ice

cream. "According to our mother, you only kind of deserve this."

I nodded my thanks and reached for the bowl. Cornelia let me take it, then stepped forward to study the picture of the box on my computer screen. "Mom's gonna go postal if she finds out you're online."

"Then we're agreed," I said, ignoring Cornelia. "We won't post a photo on the website, but we'll try to figure out together how the box works."

Nia snorted. "When, exactly, do you propose we do that? According to my mom, I've got twenty minutes after the last bell rings to get home or I'm grounded."

My mother had basically said the same thing to me over dinner. "Lunch?" I offered.

"I could do that," Nia said.

"Not me," Callie sighed. "Mrs. Watson just assigned me to give Ryan Lewis extra math help at lunch all week."

I'd never had any strong feelings about Ryan Lewis, who's in my bio class and who I ran track with last year. But at the thought that he was going to be getting forty-five minutes alone with Callie every day for a week, I suddenly found myself hating the guy for no good reason.

"What's that picture?" asked Cornelia, who doesn't wait for you to get off the phone before she asks you a question. She was pointing at the screen.

I held up a finger to ask her to give me a second. "Look, I'll think of something, okay? Give me twenty-four hours."

"How's twelve?" Nia countered.

"Fifteen."

"Done," Nia capitulated. There was a voice in the background and Nia said, "Gotta go."

"Bye, guys," said Callie.

"Bye," I said, and we all hung up.

Cornelia was bent over my desk, her nose practically touching the computer screen. "Why don't you want to post this?"

I hesitated. Was I really going to tell her that Callie, Nia, and I were in possession of a box that a group of dangerous, possibly violent people might be after? But it wasn't like she didn't know what we were up against. Like I said, Cornelia's basically a computer genius—we'd relied on her to set up theamandaproject.com, to deal with all the snags we'd hit when people logged on to tell us their Amanda stories. So she was in pretty deep already. Was the situation with the box really going to freak her out?

"We went to Play It Again, Sam," I started, and I explained everything that had happened since that morning. I couldn't bring myself to tell her about seeing our family on Thornhill's computer, though. Instead, I just finished by asking as casually as I could, "Hey, it's no big deal, but if I needed to log on to Thornhill's laptop, you couldn't help me with that by any chance, could you?"

Cornelia didn't crack a smile, but it was clear she found my attempt to be nonchalant tremendously amusing. "No big deal? You just 'happen' to want access to Vice Principal Thornhill's computer? The guy in a coma in the ICU? The guy whose office is a crime scene?"

I forced a smile. "Just a little practical joke involving a password and his Facebook account."

She raised her eyebrow at me, glanced at the computer screen one last time, then turned to go.

"Hey," I called. "There hasn't been any post on the site from a woman named Frieda, has there?" Frieda Levinson was the artist Amanda had taken me to meet in Baltimore, the reason she'd insisted our cutting school was educational enough to be called a field trip. Ever since Callie, Nia, and I had followed up on the stories Amanda had told us about her family life only to discover that Amanda might not even *have* any parents, the few adults we *did* know existed had taken on extra importance. I'd left messages on Frieda's voice mail, but she hadn't called me back, and the phone number for the studio where Amanda had taken me to see Frieda's art had been disconnected. I'd hoped she would get in touch with us via the website.

Cornelia shook her head. "Sorry," she said. "There were lots of posts, but I don't remember one from anyone named Frieda. You can check if you want—maybe I missed it."

"Maybe," I said. "Thanks."

I watched as she left the room, closing the door behind her, then spun slowly around in my chair, staring at the ceiling. *Bennett, Cornelia. Bennett, Henry. Bennett, Katharine. Bennett, Edmund.*

My whole family listed on Thornhill's file. Amanda's stuff showing up at Louise's. The box. Everything we'd discovered only seemed to make our way forward more confusing. Should

I try to remember the names on Thornhill's computer? Or would it make more sense to try to track down Frieda? I could study the photos of Amanda's box that Callie had emailed me—maybe with a little patience, they'd reveal something.

As I dropped my head in exhaustion from thinking in circles, I saw my guitar leaning against the wall in its case. I'd convinced the band to play the Lowdowners' "Baby Get Aboard My Plane" for the talent show, and I could barely pick my way through the chords. My backpack was on my bed. In it was the bio lab due on Wednesday that I hadn't even started, not to mention the two-page history essay ("How was the Treaty of Versailles unfair to Germany?") and I'd barely written the intro.

I half stood, about to grab my bag. But as I reached for it, I thought about my dad, standing all by himself even at his own parties. Before Amanda came along, I was on a track to be just like him—not necessarily lonely, but definitely alone. Now, thanks to Amanda, I had Callie and Nia. Amanda had . . . well, not to be melodramatic, but she saved me from a solitude that I could now see was a kind of life in death.

And now it was my turn to save her.

It was no contest. Dropping back down, I turned to my computer and logged on to theamandaproject.com, hoping somebody, somewhere, would know something about Amanda that could help us.

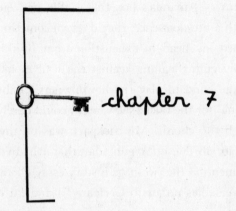

chapter 7

Seeing Callie and Nia leaning against the wall opposite the main office first thing the next morning gave me the feeling I wasn't the only one who'd spent the ride to school fantasizing about getting into Thornhill's office. Of course, Callie's prompt announcement confirmed it—no need to ponder this one.

"It's not like being closer to his *office* gets us closer to his *computer*," she pointed out. There were dark circles under her eyes, and I wondered if she had slept as little as I had.

"Actually, it does. Literally," Nia corrected her.

Callie shot Nia a look, then put her hands up in mock surrender. "Not to change the subject," she said, changing the subject, "but I brought the box." She indicated the bulging backpack slung over her shoulder.

"Not that we have any time to look at it," Nia said.

"Okay! Enough with the pressure. I've still got a few hours

to come up with a plan," I reminded her. Talking about time made me think of Amanda's watch.

I know you (x2) know me.

Was there anything in my life that *wasn't* a mystery I was not equipped to solve?

The warning bell rang and Callie gave one last, longing glance in the direction of Thornhill's office. Her voice wistful, she said, "I seem to remember a time when my life didn't center around attempts to break into administrative offices here at good old Endeavor."

"Yeah, but you weren't really happy back then," I reminded her, smiling.

She smiled back. "So true," she agreed.

And with that, the three of us headed off to our first-period classes.

At lunch, as Nia and I tried to think of a way to spend quality time together examining the box, she was kind enough not to remind me that my fifteen hours were almost up.

Desperate, I suggested the obvious. "What if we tell our parents we're going over to Callie's to study for . . . I don't know, a major ninth-grade, um, history . . . thing."

Nia started shaking her head even before I finished. "My mom would just say we should study at my house. And"— she continued when I started to interrupt—"it would take her about one minute to figure out something was up, after which I could expect to be grounded for the rest of the year, if not my life. So, you know, if you want to risk it . . ." she finished with a shrug, and I figured I should take her word

for it. Considering my mom would have my head on a platter if she got a whiff of what we were up to, I could only
imagine what Nia's notoriously strict parents would do if
they knew.

Then again, maybe I couldn't fathom it. I remembered how
old-school they'd been the one time I was there. When Cisco
Rivera, the most popular guy in the junior class (and possibly
the entire school—if not the entire *town*), started to use his
big fork on his salad, his mom clapped her hands twice and
said, "Cisco!" and when Cisco saw what she was looking at, he
changed forks so fast it was like the big one was on fire. I don't
normally think of myself as rude, but that lunch was still the
only time in my life I've actually uttered the words "No, sir"
when someone's dad asked me a question.

"Look," said Nia, "maybe we should each take it for a day
or two, see what we find, then get together with it and compare notes." She took a bite of her sandwich, and as if eating
her mother's incredible food had reminded her of her mom in
general, she added, "I'm sure I could hide it from my mom for
a *day*."

I actually wasn't so sure about my own mom—even when
she's ostensibly not looking for them, my mom has a weird
sixth sense when it comes to finding things I've hidden. For
example, the time four years ago when she suddenly had the
urge to do our family's seasonal wardrobe change the very
day I'd secretly stashed Danny Martin's water gun (no guns
allowed in the Bennett household) in my sweater drawer. Her
contraband-related ESP was so keen that I always carried

Amanda's watch with me. But it wasn't the reason I didn't like Nia's idea that we try to open the box alone.

"I feel like we need to be together to open it." Shaking my head, I added, "I know that sounds crazy."

Nia answered quickly. "No, it's fine." Her response was so immediate I was positive she and Callie had talked privately about my "feelings" since the little incident at Play It Again, Sam. My theory that Amanda's name wasn't Valentino hung between us, but Nia didn't mention it and neither did I.

"Enough about the box for a second—we're beating our heads against a brick wall with that." Nia seemed eager to change the subject. "Let's talk about Thornhill's list."

I did my best to conjure the list for Nia. Since last night, I'd started to think I might have seen Frieda's name on it, but I couldn't be sure if my thinking about Frieda had just made me *imagine* I'd read her name there or if I really had. As I recited the names I was pretty sure I'd seen, I couldn't decide which was worse: trying and failing to remember who had been on Thornhill's list, or picturing Callie and Ryan sitting in the library, heads together, laughing over some difficult-to-solve math problem. *Callie, you've made everything so clear to me. I think I'm in love with you. Oh, Ryan, you're so impossibly dense. You obviously can't function without me. I think I'm in love with you, too.*

Okay, this had to stop. With everything at stake, I had bigger things to worry about than Callie's peer-tutoring session. Still, ever since I'd seen her and Lee Forrest pass each other in the hallway without speaking, I couldn't help wondering if maybe I had a chance. . . .

The last place I would've expected to have my problem solved was art class, yet that was exactly where the solution appeared.

"Hey, Hal," said Mr. Varma. He stood behind my shoulder and looked at my still life of a bottle of Heinz ketchup and a plate with a crumpled napkin and half-eaten pickle on it. I was working from a photo I'd taken when my mom, Cornelia, and I had gone to the Orion diner for dinner a couple of weeks—or was it a lifetime?—ago.

In spite of everything that was on my mind, I'd gotten totally into the painting. As I stood in front of the canvas, the familiar feel of the brush in my hand and the soft swish of the paint had put me in a trance that took me a million miles away from the rest of my life.

"Hey," I answered. Back in September, I hadn't liked Mr. Varma as a teacher because he doesn't say much and I felt like I needed him to be more direct when he gave an assignment. By now, I'd come to see it was just a matter of listening closely to the few things he *does* say.

"I like this." He pointed at the napkin I'd worked so hard to make look crumpled.

"Thanks. I feel like the pickle isn't right, though." He looked at the misshapen object I'd drawn and frowned in concentration.

"Needs some work," he agreed. "You might want to vary the color a bit."

He was right. The shape wasn't the problem so much as its intense *greenness*. I nodded and he turned to leave, but before he could take a step away, he snapped his fingers and turned back to me.

"I have a favor to ask."

The last time Mr. Varma had asked me for a favor, I'd ended up carting dozens of canvases to the art room from a supply closet on the other side of the school. I steeled myself to hear his request.

"Eleanor is a bit . . . concerned about some of the detail work on the *As You Like It* sets."

It's so weird when teachers refer to each other by their first names; at first, I had no idea who Mr. Varma was talking about, and then I realized Eleanor must be Ms. Garner.

"Oh," I said, not sure where this was going but anticipating carrying something extremely heavy to a galaxy far, far away.

"She asked if I knew someone who could help her with a leaf situation, and I immediately thought of you."

"A *leaf* situation?" I asked.

"As in, things that do not currently look like leaves but need to be made to look like leaves in the very, very near future." He smiled wryly.

"When does she want my help?"

"After school—now that we have this security issue, they're working on sets during play rehearsal. I gather it's a bit chaotic."

I probably would have said yes to Mr. Varma anyway, but his next question guaranteed I'd be spending my afternoons happily repairing the foliage of the sets for the Forest of Arden.

"You don't happen to know anyone who could help with costumes, do you?" he added as an afterthought.

63

And suddenly, I knew that all our problems were over. "As a matter of fact, I totally do."

"I hate to break it to you, Hal, but not all girls know how to sew." Nia's arms were crossed, and her face was the picture of disdain.

I'd thought Nia would be thrilled at the news that I'd found a way for us all to hang together after school, but when I'd grabbed her at her locker, she hadn't looked especially pumped by my announcement that she and Callie were now on the *As You Like It* costume crew.

"Who said anything about sewing?" I asked, trying not to let my exasperation show as we made our way down the corridor toward Callie's locker.

"Oh, I'm sorry, I could have sworn you said the words 'costume crew.'" Nia put air quotes around the phrase.

My irritation was impossible to hide. "This is a brilliant solution," I snapped.

I spotted Callie ahead of us, and I had to call to her four or five times to be heard above the din of the crowded hallway. She waited for me and Nia to catch up. As we headed toward her, a delivery guy carrying what looked like a bouquet of flowers or maybe a plant entered through the main doors.

"Get ready to say, 'Thank you, Hal,'" I said in response to Callie's questioning look.

Nia snorted.

"Ignore that," I instructed. Callie fell into step beside me and Nia as we made our way across the lobby. "How would *you* like to have hours every day after school to sit with me and Nia and study Amanda's box?" I made my voice deep and enthusiastic, like a sports announcer's. Ahead of us, the flower delivery guy entered the main office.

"How would you like to spend hours every day *sewing*?" Nia corrected. "Isn't that right, Hal?"

We were across the hallway from the main office. Even though I hadn't been consciously heading there, I stopped walking. "Costume crew doesn't mean *sewing*!"

"I have no idea why you guys are even talking about costume crew," Callie interjected, "but I'm pretty sure the whole point of it *is* sewing."

Okay, why were they making this so impossible? "No, it's . . . you know, what you guys were doing at the store yesterday. You guys love that stuff. Like . . ." I mimed holding up a dress in front of myself.

Callie and Nia exchanged a look that clearly said: HAL IS IMPAIRED.

"I'm pretty sure it's more like . . ." Nia mimed pulling a piece of thread through a piece of fabric.

"Well, can't you . . ." I mimicked her sewing. ". . . for a couple of afternoons if it means we get some time alone together?"

Nia turned to Callie. "Hal's brilliant plan is that we join costume crew to work on Amanda's box during rehearsals."

Callie looked to me to confirm what Nia had just said, and I nodded. Then she turned to Nia. "And you object?"

"Don't you?" Nia was indignant.

Callie shrugged. "I don't know. I mean, it's not like he's asking me to sew a button on his shirt or anything."

"Oh, let me be the first to assure you both that no one would wear a shirt on which I'd sewn a button." Nia gestured at the bright brass buttons that closed the short red sweater she was wearing. "Notice what you can accomplish by calling in a professional."

"That's what my mom says about cooking!" I agreed, and just at that minute, Mrs. Leong poked her head out of the main office door.

She squinted at us, like she doubted we were who she thought we were. "I was sure I'd have to go looking for the three of you, and here you are." Was this a bad thing? Had Officer Marciano made a return trip? I had a second to feel my neck tightening with anxiety before she announced, "Callie, Hal, Nia, I have a delivery here for the three of you."

We looked at one another. What the—

"Amanda," Nia whispered.

My heart hammering in my chest, I followed the girls into the main office. On the counter in front of Mrs. Leong's desk was the pink-wrapped package the delivery guy had been carrying. Stapled to it was a plain purple envelope with

HAL BENNETT, CALLIE LEARY, NIA RIVERA

written across the front in Amanda's distinctive capital letters.

The last message she'd given the three of us together had been the postcard she'd ripped into sections and slipped into our lockers two Saturdays ago while we were sitting in detention. It was all I could do not to grab the package, hug it to my chest, and sprint to safety.

Luckily, Callie got to the package first. "Thank you so much, Mrs. Leong," she said, not reaching for it. Her voice was calm, as if there were nothing the least bit remarkable about our receiving a package at Endeavor.

Mrs. Leong was not so casual. Biting her lip, she put one hand on the package and the other on the counter. "Students don't normally receive deliveries at school. I'm not sure if . . ." She briefly glanced toward the vice principal's door, like she'd forgotten she couldn't ask Mr. Thornhill about the proper protocol in this situation.

Smiling from ear to ear, Callie leaned toward Mrs. Leong and whispered something in her ear. As she listened to Callie, Mrs. Leong broke out into a wide grin, something I'd never seen her do before.

"Really?" she asked.

Callie nodded and shrugged as if to say, *Aw shucks.*

Mrs. Leong handed her the package, then looked at me and Nia as if she wished she could hug us to her. "Well, let me just say that you three are extremely sweet."

Nia tried to hide her confusion behind an uncomfortable-looking smile-grimace combo platter, and I'm sure my expression wasn't much more natural. Fortunately, Mrs. Leong took our reactions as embarrassment rather than bewilderment.

"Let me know what she says," Mrs. Leong ordered.

"Oh, I will," Callie assured her, and a second later we were on the other side of the office door, Endeavor's end-of-day chaos surrounding us.

As Nia struggled to rip the purple envelope from the package, I asked Callie what she'd told Mrs. Leong.

"Oh, you know, just that Ms. Garner was having a hard time and we'd agreed to join the costume crew and do set design and we'd ordered her a little present to let her know how confident we were that the play's going to be a hit." She grinned with pleasure at her own subterfuge.

"Nice," I told her.

"My god," Nia muttered, teeth clenched as she pulled at the card, "this is, like, nailed on."

"The trick to a good lie is to keep it as close to the truth as possible," Callie explained, shouting to be heard over the crowd.

"I'll keep that in mind," I shouted back.

"Got it!"

Callie and I were huddled on either side of her, and as Nia slipped the card from the envelope, I didn't need psychic abilities to know how desperate we all were to see what it would say.

But what it said was . . . nothing.

There was the familiar coyote stamp in the top left-hand corner, but not a word written on the card. Nia flipped it over, then back, like maybe she'd missed some writing at first glance.

You could practically hear our disappointment.

"What the—" Nia started, but Callie interrupted her.

"Inside."

"What?" asked Nia.

"The message. It's inside."

Nia slapped her forehead, and as Callie held the package, the two of us shredded the nauseatingly bright pink paper.

I don't know what I'd expected to find inside, but it definitely wasn't the tacky FTD bouquet-in-a-basket that lay within. The flowers were so horrible they were like an affront to flowers everywhere—brightly dyed blue daisies, pink chrysanthemums, and some other orange flower I didn't recognize. In the middle of the floral abomination was a plastic sign that read GET WELL SOON in gold script.

It was like Amanda had gone out of her way to pick the ugliest bouquet in the world.

The three of us studied the arrangement, not speaking. Finally, Nia broke the silence.

"That's it?" she asked, and her eyes flashed angrily. "A get-well-soon bouquet."

"An *ugly* get-well-soon bouquet," Callie corrected her.

"Well, maybe the idea is the flowers are so repulsive they'll make you sick enough to need a get-well bouquet." Nia's voice was harsh with disappointment.

It was true—this was a relentlessly awful bouquet. I thought back to the delicate daisy chain Amanda had woven that morning in the woods. Would the person who made that have chosen such a revolting display? Then again, the card and the handwriting meant it was clearly from her.

Nia took a step back, folded her arms, and frowned at the flowers.

"I'm going to say something."

"Okay," said Callie.

"And it's going to sound crazy," she continued.

"Which would make it different from most of what we say to each other because . . . ?" I offered.

"This is a message." Nia was still staring at the depressing basket of flowers.

"Now you sound like me," I observed.

Nia looked over the flowers at me and raised an eyebrow, then made the plunge. "Who do we know who's sick?"

Callie shook her head slowly. "No one."

Nia corrected herself. "I don't mean sick like ill. I mean sick like in the hospital."

The perfect rightness of Nia's point was so powerful it hit me like a punch. This bouquet *was* a caricature. It was a caricature of the kind of bouquets people send to people who are in the hospital. Which meant . . .

"Thornhill," Callie and I whispered at the same time. We both stared at Nia, wide-eyed with amazement.

"Thornhill," she echoed, nodding her approval of our answer. "Amanda wants us to pay a visit to Thornhill."

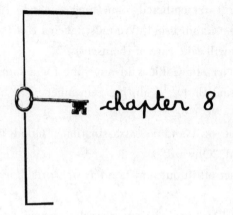

chapter 8

There's lying by omission and lying by commission, and even though I'm pretty sure the latter is worse, when I called my mom and told her I had agreed to help Ms. Garner with the sets, there was cold comfort in the fact that I was actually doing that, just not at this particular moment. True, I never actually uttered the sentence, *The reason I am not coming directly home after school is because I am staying late to help with set design*, but that was the kind of hair-splitting that carried more weight in a court of law than it would in the court of Katharine Bennett. The sheepish look on Nia's face after she slapped her phone shut said she felt totally shifty about playing fast and loose with the truth, too.

We walked to the bike racks in guilty silence. "It's all in the service of the greater good," Callie assured us as we unlocked our bikes.

"The end justifies the means," Nia agreed, throwing one leg over her bike.

Suddenly I remembered something Amanda had once quoted to me. "Gandhi said, 'We must take care of the means and the ends will take care of themselves.'"

Neither Nia nor Callie said anything for a minute, and then Callie said flatly, "Yeah, but remember what happened to him?"

I thought of Gandhi's assassination. "Good point," I acknowledged. "Onward!"

And we set off in our now-familiar single-file line.

Orion General Hospital is a surprisingly big medical complex for such a small town, and it took us a while to find the main entrance even following the instructions of the signs posted everywhere. We locked up our bikes at the crowded bike rack just outside the enormous, slowly revolving door, and Callie was about to step into it when I put a hand on her shoulder and pulled her back.

"Wait a sec," I said.

She turned to me, a confused look on her face.

"I think we need some kind of story about why we're here." For a minute, I wondered if I was being paranoid, but then I thought about why *Thornhill* was here.

Probably I wasn't being paranoid enough.

"Let's say we're his kids," Nia suggested. "And we're bringing him this." She reached into her backpack and pulled out the bouquet, which was only slightly the worse for wear.

"It's not a *total* lie," Callie said. "We *are* his kids."

"But we're not his *children*," I pointed out.

"A minor discrepancy," Nia assured me, and a second later, we'd swished through the revolving door and into the overheated, antiseptic-smelling lobby.

Our story served us well on the first floor, where a tired-looking woman with crispy red curls issued us passes that read NIA THORNHILL, CALLIE THORNHILL, and HAL THORNHILL. Even though it was just a sticker, wearing the name tag made me feel like a different person, as if I really were Vice Principal Thornhill's son. I wondered what Hal Thornhill was like. Did he win spelling bees? Have to serve detention when he missed his curfew? I imagined him bouncing a quarter on his bed after he made it, then nodding with satisfaction at the tightly pulled bedspread.

"So, what, are we triplets?" asked Callie as we rode up to his floor in the slow-moving elevator. I could tell from her voice that she was nervous, and I reached over to take her hand. Her warm fingers slid easily into mine and she gave me a gentle squeeze that I read as *Thanks*.

"If we get to the point where they want to know our birth order, we've got bigger troubles than whether or not we're triplets," Nia answered.

The number on the panel switched from two to three and the elevator gave a small ding as it stopped. A second later, the doors slid open and we were looking down a corridor at a wall with a sign that read CRITICAL CARE UNIT with an arrow beneath it pointing straight ahead. My mom, who's addicted to this show about doctors so busy flirting with one another and making witty, snappy comebacks that they can barely find the time to save lives, would have known whether critical care was better or worse than intensive care. To my ears, critical and intensive both sounded pretty awful.

Nia put her hand on my arm and I looked over at her as the three of us stepped into the corridor. "I just want to make one thing clear, okay?" she asked. Her voice was deadly serious.

Callie and I nodded.

"If it should come to it," she said, pointing at her chest, "I'm the oldest." She let go of my arm and started walking down the corridor, adding, "I am sooo tired of being someone's little sister, you have no idea," before she pushed through a pair of swinging doors marked CRITICAL CARE UNIT in six-inch-high letters.

On the other side of the doors was a large open area with numbered doors leading off it. Ahead of us was a circular nurses' station with no nurses. The space was hushed, only the occasional beep or whir of a machine. Immediately to our left was room 334, the name ATWOOD, C. on a small tag next to the room number. The next room was 333, and this one had two names, KNIGHT, E. and FELTZ, L. Our passes said THORNHILL, R. CRIT CARE, 330, and I was starting to think maybe we'd just be able to walk into Thornhill's room without having to utter the lie "our dad" again when a nurse walking at a brisk pace emerged from a room on the other side of the waiting area.

She couldn't have been much older than we were, and she looked more like an Endeavor cheerleader than a medical professional. Her blond ponytail was high up on the back of her head, and when she saw the three of us standing there, she gave us a bright smile.

"Well, *hello* there!" Her voice was chipper. There would have been nothing surprising to me if she'd added, *Give me an E!* and waved a pair of pom-poms madly in the air.

My mom's always saying people are like books and you can't judge by the cover, but come on—if this woman was the only thing between us and Vice Principal Thornhill, we were so at his bedside.

"Hi," I said, smiling at her.

"Hi!" she sang back, her white-toothed smile growing, if possible, even wider. "Can I help you? Oh, that is just the *nicest* bouquet."

I could practically hear Nia smirking beside me. "We're here to see our dad," Callie said.

The woman's blue eyes widened with sympathy. "Now, aren't you three just the sweetest?" She squeezed her shoulders and face with pleasure at our sense of filial responsibility. "Tell me, honey, what's your dad's name?"

I wasn't sure if I was the honey she was referring to, but I answered anyway. "Mister—" I began, but Nia cut me off.

"Roger Thornhill," she said, taking the flowers from Callie and holding them out as evidence of our good intentions.

For a second it seemed to me that something changed behind the sympathetic mask the nurse's face had become, and I wondered if Mr. Thornhill might be sicker than we'd thought. Maybe he was even . . . But then she was walking over to the nurses' station, murmuring, "Let me just make sure now's a good time." She picked up a phone and dialed it, speaking softly into the receiver. She listened briefly, then hung up and came over to where we were standing.

"Have a seat," she urged, still grinning broadly. Then she came over and stood so close to us that for a second I had the crazy idea that she was going to pull us into a group hug. Instead, she kind of urged us backward until we were up against a row of seats lining the wall between rooms 333 and 334. The back of one of the plastic chairs pressed into my calf, and without actually deciding to, I found myself sitting down. Next to my head was a clear plastic box, and when I turned to look at it, I saw it was emblazoned with the words IN CASE OF EMERGENCY, LIFT COVER, PRESS BUTTON. Beneath the plastic was a red button, and I wondered with a shudder what kind of emergency would be so dire you'd need more help than you could find in the Critical Care Unit.

The nurse went back to her station, and I realized that once again, Nia, Callie, and I were sitting together and waiting to see Mr. Thornhill. I thought of the expression Amanda loved to quote: *Plus ça change, plus c'est la même chose.*

The more things change, the more they stay the same.

The nurse busied herself behind the counter that hid the surface of the desk from us. Her eyes never once looked in our direction, and at first I thought she was just very engrossed in her work, but after a few minutes her focus started to seem . . .

unnatural somehow. Like she wasn't *not* looking at us so much as she was *trying* not to look at us. I told myself I was being crazy. She was a nurse. She probably had a dozen people to keep alive. Surely this woman had more important things to think about than three high school kids waiting to see their "father."

Still, I couldn't shake the feeling that something weird was going on. I glanced over at Callie and Nia, but it was hard to know if the tense expressions on their faces were the result of anything more than the fact that we'd just lied our way into a hospital to see a man who may have been attacked by the very people who caused our friend to go on the lam.

Slowly, slowly, not letting on to either of them what I was doing and keeping my movements so tiny I was sure they must be imperceptible, I began to get to my feet.

Neither Callie nor Nia noticed my movement, but no sooner had I lifted my butt off the chair than the nurse, who'd ostensibly been engrossed in her typing, shot to her feet. "Can I help you with something?" Her smile was as broad as ever, but something about it suddenly felt less enthusiastic and more . . . menacing than it had earlier. Her hand, I saw, was back on the phone and I started to get a very, very bad feeling about having judged this particular book by its peppy cover.

"You know, maybe now's not the best time to see him," I said. I put my hand under Nia's elbow and practically lifted her to her feet.

And then three things happened simultaneously.

"What are you—" Nia demanded, nearly dropping the

77

flowers as she pulled her arm away.

"You have a seat now!" snapped the nurse, lifting the receiver to her ear.

"Well, well, well, if it isn't the Thornhill children," said a voice, and we turned to see that a doctor had just walked through the doors we'd come in earlier.

And with him was a hospital guard.

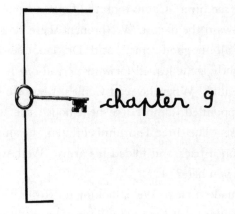

chapter 9

"Here they are, Dr. Plummer," said the nurse, and she clapped her hands together and gave a tiny jump of excitement.

"Thank you so much," said the doctor, and he came over to the three of us. He was a small man, maybe five six or so, with grayish-blond hair and glasses. Between his lab coat, the manila folder he held tucked under his arm, his pale hair, and his silver-rimmed glasses, he gave an impression of being almost completely white; I had the feeling I could pass him in a corridor and not even realize there was anyone there.

"So, you've come to see your father." His voice was chilly but he grinned broadly, as if there was nothing he liked more than meeting the families of patients in the critical care ward.

Nia stood up. "Are you his doctor?" she non-answered.

Dr. Plummer swung his eyes from me to Nia. "I might be," he said. There was something scary about the contrast between his cold voice and his bright smile, almost like he was two people in one body.

"Can we see him?" Callie took the flowers from Nia and held them toward the doctor. "We brought these."

"Mmm, all in good time," said Dr. Plummer, and he squinted slightly as he leaned forward to read our name tags. "Nia. Hal. Callie." When he read Callie's, his voice sounded slightly disappointed, almost like he'd hoped she would be somebody else. "The three Thornhill children," he announced. Then he stepped back and folded his arms. "Well, well, well. What brings you here?"

"We've made it clear. We're looking for Roger Thornhill," Nia said. I wondered if her saying Roger Thornhill instead of "our dad," meant she, too, had the feeling the jig was up.

"Yes, yes," Dr. Plummer agreed. "You three do spend a great deal of time *looking*, don't you? Looking for people."

I felt as if my body had been dipped in ice water.

"What?" Callie gasped.

"What's your point?" Nia's voice was sharp and she took a step toward the doctor. To my amazement, the guard, who had stationed himself by the door, took a step forward.

Dr. Plummer waved him back. "No, no, there's no need for all this . . . fuss." He lowered his voice so he was practically whispering. "What have you found, you three?"

Nia ignored him. "Where is he?" she demanded.

"Where is *she*?" the doctor countered. His voice was a hiss of rage.

Nia seemed completely unconcerned by the doctor's anger.

"We have no idea what you're talking about," she said firmly. "We've come here to see Roger Thornhill."

"So I've been told," Dr. Plummer responded. "Unfortunately, Roger Thornhill is no longer at this hospital."

"What?!" Callie cried.

Dr. Plummer shrugged, like he was terribly sorry he couldn't help us, then crossed over to where the nurse was sitting and placed the folder he'd been carrying on the counter in front of her.

"If you could file this when you have a moment," he murmured, and she nodded. I wondered if there was some connection between the folder and Mr. Thornhill or if it concerned some other patient and he'd just happened to be carrying it when he got the news we were here.

"Has something happened to him?" Callie asked.

Dr. Plummer swung around and faced us, his face red with anger. "Why are you refusing to tell me what I want to know?"

"We have nothing to tell you." Nia was in her fighting stance, arms crossed, one foot in front of the other. "If you're not going to tell us where Roger Thornhill is, then we're leaving."

"Such *dedicated* children!" The doctor turned to the guard. "Isn't it touching, how much they love their father?"

The guard smirked but didn't speak.

Was this an emergency? Was it time to press the IN CASE OF EMERGENCY button?

"I'm so glad you're touched, *doctor*." Nia spoke the last word with such sarcasm it was like an insult.

81

Or a question.

"Oh, yes, very." Dr. Plummer squinted at us through his glasses, then took them off and began polishing them. "You know, it's a misdemeanor to impersonate a family member in order to gain access to a hospital patient." Popping his glasses back onto his face, he stared at us through them. "And I believe you've *already* spent quite enough time with Orion's finest, am I correct? I don't know that they would be particularly . . . sympathetic to *you*, for instance, Mr. Hal *Thornhill*?" His gaze settled on me, and I tried to meet it.

It was Nia who spoke. "Are you threatening us?"

Instead of being offended, Dr. Plummer laughed. But it was a creepy, bitter laugh with no sense of humor in it. "Oh, no, my dear. I would never threaten three such lovely children. I might just . . . keep an eye on them. See what they were up to."

"Talk about a *misdemeanor*!" Nia countered.

As abruptly as Dr. Plummer had started laughing, he stopped. "My dear young lady, know whose side you are on before you begin issuing legal threats." He smiled to himself at the wisdom of his observation. "Yes, indeed. We should all know whose side we are on."

A second later Dr. Plummer was walking through the double doors he'd come in, the guard close at his heels.

As soon as they were gone, Callie and I walked over to Nia and high-fived her.

"Nia," I said. "You're a total Bond girl."

"As if," Nia corrected, snapping her head around and giving me a withering stare. "More like a total Bond."

I put up my hands to indicate I'd meant no offense. Callie smiled weakly. I saw that her hand holding the bouquet was trembling.

"Here," I said. "Give me that and let's get out of here."

I reached toward the bouquet and for a second Callie seemed to be handing it to me, but then I felt her pulling it back.

"Wait!" she whispered. She glanced in the direction of the nurses' desk. "I have an idea."

"What are you—" Nia started, but she broke off when she saw the nurse was staring at us.

"I suggest you three leave. Immediately." She was standing behind her desk, grinning her freaky, cheerleader grin at us.

Barely moving her lips, Callie muttered, "Follow my lead," and the three of us shuffled toward the nurses' station. When we were a few feet away from it, Callie said loudly, "Um, we have these flowers and it seems a shame to . . ." She shrugged, then seemed to slip on an invisible spot on the scuffed floor. Her right leg shot out and as she missed her footing, she got tangled up in Nia's leg. Nia shouted as she went down. An instant later, Callie had fallen across the counter, dropping the bouquet almost onto the nurse's lap.

"You *idiots*!" screamed the nurse, looking down at her soaked uniform. "You absolute idiots!" She brushed at the water that I could literally hear dripping all over the floor.

"Oh, I am so, so sorry," Callie said. She was practically hanging over the nurses' desk. I heard the sound of tissues being pulled up from a dispenser and keys on a keyboard being depressed and released. "I think the keyboard's okay, but . . ."

"Get out of here!" the nurse exploded.

Callie backed away from the nurses' station, helping Nia to her feet as she did so. "I'm really sorry, ma'am," she said. The nurse took a step back and there was a large crunch. Callie added, "Careful of the glass!" before whispering, "Let's run."

Nia and I didn't have to be told twice. We followed Callie out the doors and down the corridor, bagging the slow-moving elevator in favor of our own foot power and the stairs. As we raced down the empty, dimly lit, cement stairwell, I had time to think of all the movies I'd ever seen in which the criminal corners the protagonist in just such an abandoned setting, when at last Callie was pushing on a door marked EXIT ONLY– NO REENTRY and we were outside in the cool Orion dusk.

"What a *waste*." I kicked angrily at the Dumpster in front of us.

"The 'she' the doctor was talking about was Amanda, wasn't it?" asked Nia. "I mean, I'm not being crazy here, right?"

"I got it," said Callie, from right behind me.

"Yeah, I figured," said Nia, her voice thick with disappointment and frustration. "We all got it. The question is—why?"

"No." Callie put one hand on Nia's shoulder and one on mine and turned us to face her. Unlike ours, her face was sparkling with excitement. "I mean, I got *it*." She reached under her thick green poncho and pulled on something.

An instant later, she was holding in front of us a manila envelope with the words *Roger Thornhill* printed on the tab.

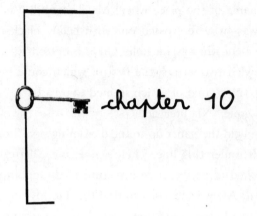

chapter 10

Nia clapped her hands and spun around on one spiky heel. "Oh my god, *you're* the Bond. I can't believe you used to spell your name with just an 'i.'"

"I'll forget you said that," said Callie, but her grin made it clear she didn't care *what* Nia said.

She flipped open the folder. It was thin enough that I hadn't exactly expected to find a novel inside, but I'd assumed there'd be a bunch of medical records and maybe some information about his next of kin or allergies to penicillin or something. Instead, there was only one piece of hospital letterhead containing three brief sentences.

"Roger Thornhill was admitted to Orion General Hospital on March 24 having suffered a TBI to his sphenoid resulting in intra-axial lesions. He was released on March 27 to Dr. Joy of Baltimore, Maryland, for further observation at his lab. Dr. Joy's initials below indicate he has possession of Mr. Thornhill's medical records."

The name of the place where Mr. Thornhill was and the town it was in were crossed out with heavy black ink. The signature beneath was illegible. On the bottom of the page were scrawled two letters, the first of which could have been anything, the second of which seemed to be a J.

"He's gone," Nia breathed.

Callie held the paper up to the darkening sky. "I can't read whatever's under this line. There's, like, not a letter visible." Callie looked at us, her face a picture of disappointment. "I don't get it. Are we supposed to find this Dr. Joy?"

"How could she even know about him? She sent us to find Thornhill," Nia countered.

"Or," Callie offered, "she sent us to find Thornhill because she knew he would lead us to Dr. Joy."

I thought of Frieda, who I hadn't heard back from, and how she, too, was in Baltimore. Was it just a coincidence that Amanda had taken me for a day trip to the same city where Dr. Joy had his lab? "Amanda knows this woman in Baltimore. An artist named Frieda. I met her once. Do you think there's a connection?"

"Then why not just send us to Baltimore to find Dr. Joy in the first place?" Nia sounded ready to weep with frustration. Both girls stared at me, their eyes seeming to beg me to do something.

But what could I do? I had no idea why Amanda had sent us the get-well-soon bouquet, why she'd left me the watch with the mysterious inscription, why Louise had given us the box we couldn't even open.

"We don't even know her last name!" I bellowed.

For the second time in my presence, Callie and Nia gave each other a Hal's-clearly-losing-it look. I'd let it go at Play It Again, Sam, but having them think I was crazy in addition to everything else that had happened that afternoon was just a little more than I could take.

"I'm outta here." I marched over to my bike and unlocked it. When Nia and Callie called my name, I swung around to face them. "I'm not crazy!" I yelled at them. And then I thought of something. "But if I am, she *made me* that way." I threw my leg over my bike and pedaled off into the rush-hour traffic as hard as I could.

Mine was definitely a dark night of the soul, and by the time I saw Callie in the theater's lobby after school, I was feeling totally embarrassed about the meltdown I'd had the previous day; when Callie greeted me like nothing had happened, I could have hugged her.

"Hey." She smiled, gesturing to her backpack. "I've got the box."

I gave her an only slightly forced thumbs-up, trying to be optimistic. Surely things had to start improving. Surely we wouldn't strike out again. By the end of today's rehearsal, we'd have discovered what was inside the box, and that would answer at least some of our questions about Amanda. I put my hand on Callie's back, and the "Great" I answered was full of hopeful enthusiasm.

Nia called out and waved to us from the other side of the lobby. Her electric-blue shirt hummed across the crowded space, and I remembered again the time when Nia Rivera had been all about blending in, disappearing into the crowd that was our grade. We made our way over to where she was standing, and when we got there, she snapped her gum once, as if chomping on those days when she'd denied herself her rightful place in the pantheon of cool. I knew it was heresy to say this, but compared to Nia, Cisco Rivera seemed to me to be just a good-looking guy who also happened to be a great athlete and decent person.

I wondered how much longer he'd be known as the "cool" Rivera sibling.

To her credit, Nia didn't refer to my storming off the previous day, either. "Okay, kids. We walk through that door, we sign in or whatever, then we sequester ourselves in the corner with *that*." She pointed toward Callie's backpack.

"Totally," Callie agreed, but I couldn't help sensing that her enthusiasm sounded a little muted.

"You okay?" I whispered as we followed Nia through the door and into the auditorium.

"Yeah, of course," Callie said quickly. "It's just . . ."

Heidi Bragg's voice boomed from the front of the theater. "Just because I'll be dressed like a boy doesn't mean I won't look hot." Sitting on the edge of the stage, she flipped her hair off her face and beamed out at the people sitting in the seats and milling around the auditorium, putting on a little pre-rehearsal show.

88

"It's . . . well, that," Callie whispered, indicating Heidi with her chin.

When I'd suggested we use play rehearsal as a way to spend time examining the box, I'd totally forgotten about Heidi's being the star of the show, but now that I remembered, I felt terrible. "God, Callie, I wasn't thinking. Why don't we . . . Just leave the box with us, okay? It's crazy for you to have to be here."

Nia stopped abruptly in the middle of the aisle, and Callie and I walked right into her.

"Hi. Klutzy much?" she asked, but the look on her face when she turned to Callie was more concerned than annoyed, and it made me wonder if she, too, had suddenly realized what our decision to meet here meant for Callie.

Nia and Heidi were ancient enemies. But with Callie and Heidi, the days-old wound hadn't begun to scar over.

"You know, Callie," Nia said, her voice way too casual to be casual, "there's no reason for you to hang out if you'd rather . . ."

Callie tossed back her curly hair in a gesture that, ironically, was not unlike Heidi's and her eyes seemed to sizzle with defiance. "What, rather go home and wait by the phone? I don't *think* so, honey."

Was it my imagination, or did she actually square her shoulders as she spoke?

At the sound of Callie's voice, Heidi's head swung in our direction. I waited for her to shout a nasty comment like the ones she'd hurled at Callie the day of the lunchroom show-down when Callie chose to sit at lunch with me and Nia rather

89

than with her now former friends, the I-Girls. Instead, Heidi gave our threesome a long, long look, then turned away without saying a word.

Far from being relieved by her silence, I felt chilled to the bone. Heidi Bragg was one scary girl. From the time I'd arrived at Orion, I'd been hearing from all the guys in our grade how Heidi Bragg was "so hot" and "super fly" but she'd always left me cold. She was great-looking, sure, but in a totally synthetic way. If you touched her, I imagined she'd feel as hard as a plastic mannequin.

"Let's go tell Ms. Garner we're here," said Nia, and in her voice I heard the decision to ignore Heidi's glare.

"So I was wrong," I hissed. "So sue me."

"Oh, I plan to, Hal Bennett. Don't you worry your pretty little head about *that*." Nia's words were muffled by the pins pressed between her lips, but they were clear enough for me to understand. A second later, she swept by me for the zillionth time in the past hour, an enormous pile of costumes laid across her arms, a train of fabric trailing behind her.

From the second we'd told Ms. Garner who we were and why we were there, she'd pressed us into immediate service. Callie and Nia were whisked away to the costume designer, home ec teacher Mrs. Hayworth, almost before we could say good-bye, and except for a brief glimpse of them as they came in and out with costumes and materials from the costume shop, I hadn't seen them since.

It wasn't like I was exactly rolling in free time myself. The

Forest of Arden that had been painted on the scrim hanging at the back of the stage looked as if it had been designed by the love child of Jackson Pollock and Georgia O'Keeffe—there were strange, elongated figures that, if you glanced at them quickly while squinting hard, almost looked like they might have once been trees. Also gigantic blobs that I supposed were bushes or maybe the huts of Ardenian gnomes (though I didn't recall from our English class's reading of the play there actually *being* gnomes in Arden).

"Hal, work your magic," Ms. Garner had murmured, her eyes slightly teary as she pulled away from the awkward embrace in which she'd clutched me. "I believe in you," she added, her voice no more than a whisper.

"Um, thanks," I muttered. When she indicated the piles of paint cans and brushes that were mine to use, I really had to hold back from asking for a blowtorch instead.

I'd spent the better part of twenty minutes trying to find someone who knew how to raise and lower the scrims, but despite there being half a dozen crew members around, everyone I asked looked with confusion at the complex system of ropes and pulleys that worked the different backdrops, finally suggesting I wait for Ms. Wisp before attempting to "mess" with stuff.

"I'm not 'messing' with stuff, I'm 'fixing' it," I finally snapped at the last person who'd promised he could help me, then shrugged his shoulders in bewilderment when I asked him how to drop the scrim to the floor.

All I wanted was to be alone somewhere, working on my painting or running through the silent afternoon. Or sitting with Callie and Nia and finally solving one tiny piece of the Amanda puzzle. Instead, I was up on a ladder, my back halfway to broken, my shoulder screaming in agony as I leaned toward the scrim and attempted to turn what looked like a green flying saucer into something remotely resembling an object found in nature.

Amanda Valentino, when we find you, I'm going to make you pay for this.

It's possible I could have ignored my physical discomfort and gotten into the fact that at least I was painting if it hadn't been for the torture of listening to Heidi Bragg butcher Shakespeare. I will fully admit I'm not one to peruse the Bard in my spare time, but the sound of his poetry had never before made me want to run screaming from the room. Heidi's overacting, her dramatic pauses, her painfully tone-deaf rendering of his soliloquies were all like a subtle form of torture, one I had no doubt the government would be glad to get its hands on. I, for one, would happily have told anyone anything I knew if it would just make Heidi stop.

Normally when I'm working I don't even notice if my phone buzzes, but now I was so glad to have something to focus on other than Heidi's voice that in my eagerness to answer the call, I dropped my brush ten feet to the ground. There was a text message, and when I opened it, I saw it was from Cornelia.

IDK IF THIS IS WHAT U WERE WAITING
FOR, BUT IT WAS JUST POSTED. IT CAME
FROM FREE2BU&ME.

FREE2BU&ME. Could that be Frieda's screen name?
The posting from FREE2BU&ME followed.

HAL, IF YOUVE BEEN LEAVING
ME VM MSGS, TXT ME W/ WHAT U BOUGHT
THE DAY WE MET IN BALTIMORE.

"Come on, you have the cool clothes, the groovy hair, the earring. You need this. It completes the look."

"Give me a break, Valentino. I don't have a 'look.'"
I shook my head at her, embarrassed. We were standing in a vintage clothing store in downtown Baltimore, and in front of her, Amanda was holding a worn biker jacket, the silver zippers gleaming against the weathered leather.

Amanda wore a tailored skirt and jacket of navy blue, and her hair was pulled back from her face in a tight, low bun. On her feet were low gray pumps, and the stockings had seams up the back. I didn't normally notice her outfits, but today she looked exactly like the pictures of my grandmother, who'd worked as a secretary (or, as she'd called it, a "Kelly girl") in New York in the 1950s.

"Hal Bennett, do you really not know you have a look?" She cocked her head at me, like she was trying to decide if I was kidding her.

"Come on," I said, pulling on her arm that wasn't holding the jacket. "Let's go meet Frieda."

Something in my voice must have convinced her I was telling the truth because she slipped her arm out of my grasp and dropped the jacket to the floor. Then, taking both my hands in hers, she looked at me for a long, long moment. "You have a look, Hal. You look like a sensitive guitar-playing painter who can run 5K in under fifteen minutes."

Despite (or maybe because of) the intensity of her gaze, I laughed. "Listen, I can't speak for the sensitive thing, but as for the rest—I don't *look* like those things, Valentino. I *am* those things."

But my joke didn't make her laugh. "Exactly," she said. Then she bent down, picked up the jacket, and slipped my arm into it.

Sometimes it was easier to humor Amanda than to fight her, and now was definitely one of those times. I let her work the jacket over my shoulder, then slipped my other arm into it. She came back to stand in front of me, untucking the collar where it had gotten twisted.

"Aah," she said, looking at me like I was something she'd made and was pleased with.

"Satisfied?" I teased.

She moved me a few paces to the left, then turned me around to face a mirror that hung on the back of a dressing-room door.

I had to admit it—the jacket made me look very, very cool. It was cut broad at the shoulders and narrow at the waist, and seeing me in it, you'd think I'd just hopped off my motorcycle and was heading to play a quick guest set with Mick and Keith.

"You've got a good eye, Valentino, I'll give you that." I forced myself to look away from that guy staring back at me in the mirror. Because there was no way around it—he was *way* cooler than I'd ever be. "Now, let's go." I started to remove the jacket.

But Amanda put her hand on my chest, stopping me.

"You're going to tell me that the clothes make the man, so I need this jacket, right?" I asked.

She shook her head slowly. "Don't you get it, Hal?"

"What?" Suddenly I didn't feel like joking anymore.

"Nature forms us for ourselves, not for others; to be, not to seem."

Now it was my turn to shake my head. "Still not getting it," I admitted.

And now she was the one who smiled. "I am saying that you need this jacket because you *don't* need this jacket."

Heart pounding, I entered Frieda's number and typed a reply.

BLACK LEATHER VINTAGE JACKET. HAL.

It seemed I'd barely hit SEND when my phone buzzed again. I flipped it open and read the new message on my screen.

I NEED TO SEE U. TAKE THE 1:42 FROM
ORION TO BALTIMORE ON SAT. MEET ME
@ THE OLD TRAIN STATION. I WILL NOT
CONTACT U AGAIN BTWN NOW & THEN.

There was one final sentence, three words long.

TELL NO ONE.

95

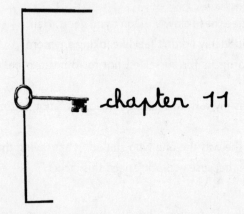

chapter 11

I went to Baltimore alone.

At first I was going to tell Callie and Nia about Frieda's text. I knew I should. I kept hearing my mom's voice:

What would you want them to do if the situation were reversed?

And of course the answer was obvious: I'd want them to tell me.

When we were walking out of school together on Friday and they started talking about how we needed to find a way to convince our parents to let us go to Baltimore so we could find Dr. Joy, I tried to change the subject. "Do you realize nobody but Thornhill seems to know we're supposed to be in Saturday detention for the car thing?"

As soon as the sentence was out of my mouth, I thought about how my dad's always saying there are no accidents. Had I mentioned our not having to serve detention out of a guilty conscience? Was part of me hoping they'd suggest we all go to Baltimore together on Saturday so that I'd have to bring them with me to meet Frieda or at least tell them about her?

If so, my plan backfired, since my mentioning Saturday provided them with the opportunity not to suggest we spend the day investigating but to remind me that *some of us* were going to be spending Saturday stuck in the theater and working on *costumes* for a certain *play* because a certain *other* somebody who shall remain *nameless* had signed them up for a certain *job* that never seemed to end, whereas that certain somebody's job did not require a Saturday shift.

"Wow, that guy sounds like a real jerk," I agreed, then hopped on my bike and hightailed it out of the parking lot.

I told myself I wasn't telling them about my trip because Frieda had been explicit in her instructions: *TELL NO ONE.*

So it wasn't like she'd *told* me to tell them and I hadn't.

I even tried to convince myself it was safer for me to go alone than to drag the girls into it (oh, yeah, because I'd so totally rescued Callie and Nia from creepy doctor guy—*not!*). I told myself all kinds of stuff, but by the time I got on the train Saturday afternoon, I was pretty sure the truth was a whole lot less altruistic.

I *wanted* to go to Baltimore alone.

I wanted to be the one who discovered the missing link to Amanda, the one who found her when no one else could. And I didn't want to share all of my memories of that day in the city, how it felt when Frieda took me seriously as an artist, how grown-up it seemed to be ordering lunch at a Baltimore diner right as the rest of my class was sitting in fourth period. That day was one of the happiest of my life, and it was also private. It was mine. Mine and Amanda's.

Wondering if that made me a total jerk, I opened the folder Cornelia had slipped into my hand as I was walking out the door earlier. I'd told her I was on my way to an afternoon rehearsal (note to self: add "lies to awesome little sister" to list of things to admire about Hal Bennett), and she gave me a sort of funny look before saying she'd printed out everything that had come into the website in the past couple of days. "I figured you and Callie and Nia might want hard copies."

At the mention of Callie and Nia, I couldn't meet Cornelia's eyes, so I just mumbled something vague, then took the pages from her and pushed the button to open the garage door and grab my bike. My mom was at a conference, learning about pursuing "nontraditional" college applicants. I couldn't help thinking she wouldn't exactly appreciate my "nontraditional" plans for the afternoon.

As the train pulled out of Orion and I flipped open Cornelia's folder, the henna tattoo of the cougar on the inside of my forearm caught my eye. I touched it lightly, thinking of all the things that had happened in the brief time since Amanda had convinced me to get it. Somehow I felt like the person who'd taught me that cougars are strong and solitary, that they stake out their territory and patrol it, would understand my needing to go to Baltimore alone.

The thought of Amanda understanding me, wherever she was, made me feel comforted somehow, and as I started flipping through the pages Cornelia had printed out, I didn't feel quite so much like the world's most selfish immature loser.

The top page was a posting from someone who thought Amanda was part of a crazy science experiment that turned her invisible, and she got stuck that way.

I chuckled and turned to the next printout—a testimonial written by a girl from a town called Saint Albans in Wyoming. She wrote that when her dad had a heart attack and it looked like he wasn't going to pull through, Amanda had spent a day and a night sitting with her outside ICU, waiting for news (he'd survived, she told us, and was helping her mother prepare dinner as she was posting).

The page after that was a post written by a girl named Poppy. She wrote that until Amanda came to her school, she was always made fun of for her patched clothing and shy personality, but when Amanda found her crying in the bathroom, she promised to make the bullying stop, which she did.

Next came something from a girl who was sure Amanda was in Kansas, because a girl who tried out for the soccer team named Amanda Valentory (obviously, she informed us, the same person as our Amanda Valentino) also painted their principal's car and then disappeared.

Shaking my head, I turned the page and found myself reading an article someone anonymously submitted about a woman named Annie Beckendorf who'd been killed in a car accident just weeks before Amanda showed up in Orion. According to the article, "Ms. Beckendorf was hit and killed by a driver in a blue Mercedes when she ran a red light at high speed in what may have been a high-velocity chase with an unidentified driver in another car." The person who'd sent in the article to theamandaproject.com had also scanned in a list of Ms. Beckendorf's personal effects, a list that, according to the letterhead, was the property of the California Medical Examiner's Office. Not really wanting to know how some random kid had hacked into the coroner's computer files, I skimmed the list, looking for anything that might hold a key to the connection between Amanda and this Annie Beckendorf woman, and it was literally a key that caught my eye. Apparently, in addition to her purse, phone, and clothing, Annie Beckendorf had in her possession at the time of her death "one antique key, silver-plated."

I thought of the small silver key Amanda always wore on a ribbon around her neck. Everything about her changed almost daily—her hair color, her style, sometimes even her accent and skin tone. But she always, *always* wore the key on the blue ribbon.

Suddenly I had an insane thought. Could Amanda have been the driver of the Mercedes? Could she have . . . killed a person accidentally and could she be on the run from her crime? If so, it would be just like her to wear a talisman to remind her of what she'd done, something that would make it impossible for her to put the accident out of her mind for even a day. Could her own guilt have been what made her realize the secret Callie was keeping, that she knew Heidi Bragg had hit Beatrice Rossiter that night while illegally test-driving her dad's car?

I didn't even realize what I was doing until I'd actually hit Callie's number on speed dial, and then I frantically pushed END CALL about a thousand times. *Hey, Callie, it's Hal. I completely lied to you and Nia about this, but I'm on my way to Baltimore and I want to run a theory by you. Is that cool?*

Anyway, Amanda didn't exactly seem like the hit-and-run type. I thought of the girl with the dad in ICU, the girl she'd supposedly sat with through a day and a night, and the girl she protected from bullies. It wasn't that you *couldn't* be a good Samaritan *and* a murderer, but I just didn't see an unlicensed Amanda stealing someone's car and committing vehicular underaged manslaughter.

Heidi Bragg, yes. Amanda, no.

Thinking of Heidi hitting Beatrice Rossiter with her dad's "borrowed" car reminded me of seeing Bea's name on Thornhill's list. Or not seeing Bea's name on the list. Which had it been, again? I flipped open my phone and texted Cornelia.

ANY LUCK GETTING INTO THORNHILLS
COMPUTER?

As if she'd been sitting and waiting for me to write to her, Cornelia texted back in less than a minute.

AM RUNNING WEBSITE (FULL-TIME JOB)
WHILE TRYING NOT 2 FAIL OUT OF SCHOOL.
SO SORRY UNABLE TO SATISFY ALL UR

MAJESTYS NEEDS IMMEDIATELY.

MY BAD,

I texted back, adding,

THANKS FOR FOLDER. V INTERESTING STUFF
HERE.

She didn't respond, too busy with other things, no doubt.

It had been overcast when I'd boarded the train in Orion, and now sheets of rain slapped against my window. It created a beautiful effect, blurring the houses and landscape we were speeding through. Out of habit, I found myself opening my sketchbook and starting to draw, but my heart wasn't in it. I realized that I missed Callie and Nia—it was weird to be on the train without them, to be looking for Amanda without them. By the time the train pulled into Baltimore, I felt like an über-moron for making the trip on my own. What did I think, that Amanda was going to magically appear on the platform of the station, that traveling in space equaled traveling in time back to that day?

I crammed all my stuff into my messenger bag and walked down the aisle toward the door. I saw a copy of Orion's alternative paper, *The Midnighter*, on the seat across from me and scooped it up, too. Amanda loved that paper; so strange to see it here. As soon as I was back in Orion, I'd tell them everything—Frieda's text, the trip to Baltimore to meet her, the printouts from Cornelia. Even the watch and its mysterious, confusing message. I smiled as I thought of Nia giving me crap for going it alone, for not being able to decipher Amanda's gift without their help. *Guess you're not the Lone Ranger after all, are you?* Did girls even know about the masked man? Or was that just something for guys and their dads? Thinking of Nia as a little kid watching old episodes of *The Lone Ranger* with her dad made me laugh out loud, and I was still smiling when I stepped off the train and into the driving rain. I pulled my hoodie up over my head and sprinted for the station, getting soaked in the few seconds I'd been exposed to the downpour.

Standing just inside the automatic doors, I opened Frieda's text and reread the instructions I'd memorized the first time I'd read them.

MEET ME @ THE OLD TRAIN STATION.

I looked around. The space I stood in was about as new as something that didn't still have the wrapping on it could be—there were shiny ticket dispensers and modular, brightly colored plastic chairs. The floor was scuffed linoleum, but I had the feeling that had happened within minutes of the station's ribbon cutting. No doubt about it, this was definitely the *new* train station.

Despite the sign over his head, the guy manning the information booth didn't seem too keen on giving out any actual information. Instead, he seemed to believe that I was some kind of bumbling lunatic put on this earth to torment him.

"Come again?" He'd been doing a sudoku puzzle when I got to the window, and it was clear that every second away from it was torture for him.

"The old station," I repeated.

"Whaddya mean, 'old'?" He scratched at his stubbly cheek, looking so confused I almost wondered if the word itself was unfamiliar to him.

Was it possible Frieda had been messing with me—just dragging me down to Baltimore to send me on some kind of wild goose chase?

But why?

I took a deep breath. "Is this a new train station?" I asked. "I mean, was it built recently?"

"You betcha," said the guy. "Two years ago." The pride in his voice made it sound like he himself had laid the cornerstone.

"So, the train station that was here *before* this one. Where's that?"

Now the guy looked at me like there was no doubt in his mind that I was completely dense. "It was here." He pointed to the ground in case I was missing the point. "We hadda tear it down to build the new one."

I have never been a violent person. My mom always says how proud she was that when I was little and other kids would take a toy from me in the sandbox, I'd never grab for it; I'd just slowly negotiate it back from them. But I swear, right at that second, I felt capable of punching in a wall.

"Yeah," the guy continued. "That's all gone now. Some developer was talkin' about turnin' the waiting room into a restaurant like, wait, waddya call it—" He turned to someone standing in the office behind him, out of my line of vision. "Hey, Eddie, what's the name of that place in New York—in, you know, Grand Central Station?" I couldn't make out Eddie's response, but Information Guy repeated it for my edification. "The Oyster Bar." He smiled and nodded at the idea. "It's a real nice space, that old waiting room, but now it's just all boarded up."

"Wait!" I almost shouted, and he scowled at my interfering with his Oyster Bar–inspired reverie. "Did you say *now*? So it's still there?"

He shook his head, and his eyes briefly looked over my head to the far side of the station. "Kid, like I said, there's really nothing there."

But I was already dashing in the direction his eyes had shown me. "Thanks!" I called over my shoulder, and I got a glimpse of him shaking his head as he pulled his sudoku puzzle back in front of him.

I don't usually ignore direct orders such as KEEP OUT, especially when they're written in letters almost a foot high. Still, desperate times call for desperate measures, and when I got to the doors I just pushed through them without even hesitating, like instead of KEEP OUT they said COME IN.

Stepping through the doors really *was* like stepping back in time. Where before the station had been all plastic, metal, and neon, here was wood and leather, a beautiful waiting room out of a different century. A huge old clock on the wall had stopped forever at five minutes past nine, and smoked glass skylights let in the gray light of the day. I could see why someone would have wanted to preserve this space—as a restaurant or a gallery or a store—anything to make sure its finely wrought metal grilles and worn wooden floor weren't ripped up for scrap.

"Hal."

I spun around. Across the room from where I'd entered stood Frieda, her head swathed in a dark scarf against the wet rainy day.

"You made it," she observed, and a moment later I'd crossed over to her and she was grabbing both of my hands, hard, in hers.

"Hi, Frieda," I said. She looked older than she had the last time we met, or maybe she was just tired. As she loosened her scarf, I saw that her salt-and-pepper hair still framed her face in a crazy, frizzy halo, but her eyes weren't quite as shiny as I remembered, and there was something about how she immediately led me over to a nearby bench that made me think she needed to sit down.

Her eyes darted nervously around the dusty, empty space. "We have so much to discuss, and I'm not sure how much time we have." She wasn't whispering, exactly, but her voice was low. I realized just how quiet it was compared to the hustle and bustle of the new station.

"You've heard from her." The sentence was out of my mouth even before I realized I was going to speak it.

Frieda's eyes suddenly bore into mine, a question as much as a look. I met her gaze, and slowly, almost imperceptibly, she nodded. My heart hammered in my chest.

"What did she—"

But Frieda cut me off before I could finish my question. "I can't tell you what she said, so don't even ask."

I remembered now just how definite Frieda could be. *Jasper Johns is the only true genius of modern art. Impressionism is so overrated it makes me want to throw up. A society that values artists as little as ours does gets what it deserves.*

There'd been no arguing with her at lunch that day, and there was no arguing with her now. But that was okay—there were other questions I had to ask.

"Frieda, what do you know about Dr. Joy?"

If Frieda had looked tired before, suddenly she was on high alert. Her nose practically quivered with amazement. "What do *you* know about Dr. Joy?" she countered.

"He—" Suddenly I realized I didn't even know for sure Dr. Joy *was* a he—god, Nia would have *killed* me for making such a sexist assumption. "*Or* she," I self-corrected, "has a lab here in Baltimore. He signed our vice principal, Mr. Thornhill, out of Orion General."

Frieda folded her hands together and pressed them against her chin. For a moment, she was silent, as if weighing what she wanted to tell me. When she spoke, she said simply, "Dr. Joy is a man. And you can't find him now."

How could Frieda possibly be so sure? We'd *seen* the paperwork with our own eyes. He had a lab right here in Baltimore. "Of course we can. He's—"

Frieda raised her voice only slightly, but her announcement

silenced me. "Joy's lab was dismantled extremely suddenly two days ago. He's gone into hiding."

Facts were coming at me too fast for me to respond. It was like swimming against a powerful riptide. "But—Callie and Nia and I, we *saw* the letter signing him—"

Now it was Frieda's turn to look shocked. "Callie, you, and Nia?" She reached across the space that separated us and grabbed my shoulder. I was surprised by the strength of her grip. "What were you doing together?" There was something in her voice that made her seem . . . panicked.

Her anxiety confused me. Had we done something wrong? "What were we doing together?" I repeated. "We were looking for Amanda." Frieda had found me through the website. She must have seen Nia's and Callie's names there as well.

Letting go of my shoulder, Frieda dismissed my explanation with a wave of her hand. "Yes, I know that you're looking for her. But are you saying you were together at the hospital?"

"Of course we were." Did Frieda think the three of us were, like, just virtual friends, people who hung out together online but never in the actual world?

To herself, Frieda muttered, "I had no idea . . ." and then she was clutching my hand again, her voice urgent. "Don't you know it's dangerous for the three of you to be together? When you're together you're—"

Far off, we both heard a sound, like a pile of paint cans or some other stacked metal had toppled over. Our eyes met, and I could see my own thought mirrored in Frieda's face.

That noise did not come from the new station.

For a long moment, neither of us so much as breathed. Then, so quietly it took me a second to even realize she was speaking, Frieda began whispering at breakneck speed. "Go back to the station. Stay in a crowded area. Get on the first train headed for Orion and board a car with as many other people as possible."

"Wait!" My voice was pitched as low as hers. "What were you going to say? Why is it dangerous for us to be together?"

Again a sound, this time of a circular piece of metal spinning, spinning, and finally coming to rest on a wooden floor.

"Go!" she hissed. "And don't look for Dr. Joy anymore. They've got him. I'm sure of it."

"But, Frieda, what about you? I can't just leave you here."

She pulled me to my feet, turned me toward the door, and literally pushed me back in the direction from which I'd come.

"I know how to disappear. Now run."

The time for questions had passed. It was time to start following orders.

I ran.

chapter 12

They've got him.

It's dangerous for you to be together.

They've got him.

It's dangerous for you to be together.

The whole ride back to Orion, the wheels of the train seemed to churn out the rhythm of Frieda's warnings until my own heart actually seemed to beat along with her words. I remembered Amanda's final note to Thornhill, the reference to danger, her plea for help.

What the hell was going on here?

My fingers shaking, I dialed Callie's number, but as soon as I heard the outgoing message on her voice mail, it was all I could do not to hang up. *It's dangerous for you to be together.* What part of dangerous did I not understand? Was I seriously going to put Callie and Nia in danger just because I needed to share, spread the wealth?

"Hey, it's Callie. Leave me a message." Hearing her voice made me see the red of her hair, smell her shampoo or perfume or laundry detergent that made me think of a sunny April morning whenever I smelled it.

Was I going to put that in danger?

"Um, hey, Callie, it's, um, Hal. I . . . guess that . . . I'll see you. On Monday. In play rehearsal. So, bye." My message was so random and disjointed even the woman sitting across from me raised an eyebrow in disdain as I flipped my phone shut and shoved it into my pocket. It was all I could do not to shout at her, *Hey, lady, my friend's life might be in danger if I talk to her, so maybe you could excuse me for panicking over here, all right?* Instead, I turned my head and stared out at the sky, so gray it was almost black. What had appeared beautiful on the way down now felt ominous. I thought of everything that might be hiding beyond the brightly lit windows of my train car and shuddered.

If we were in danger when we were together, did that mean we were safe when we were apart? The question formed itself in my mind as I rode my bike home, glad for the first time ever that there was no way to get from my house to the train station without traveling the busy streets of downtown Orion.

This was insane. I had to tell Callie and Nia what had happened. I tried them both but neither picked up, and *We might be in serious danger* isn't exactly a message you leave on a voice mail. I figured I'd call later, but then my mom came home ranting about how she and Cornelia and I were going to watch *The Philadelphia Story* together because driving home from the conference she'd realized neither of us had ever seen it and that was, like, a criminal offense. By the time we'd eaten and watched the movie, Callie and Nia must have been asleep because both their cells went right to voice mail. I got in bed and lay there not sleeping, for hours. Finally, just as the sky was getting light, I dozed off.

When I woke up it was after ten. Without even getting out of bed, I texted Callie and Nia.

CAN U COME OVER TODAY?

I went downstairs. There was a note from my mom—

Good morning, sleepyhead.
Cornelia and I went
to breakfast. Will
bring you muffins
from Rosie's.
Love, Mom

Rosie's was this total old-school diner where my family went a lot. Thinking about their Belgian waffles was enough to tempt me to hop on my bike and meet my mom and my sister downtown.

Half planning to get dressed and head out, I walked past

the den. It's supposed to be a home office for both my parents: In the corner is a desk with a computer and a filing cabinet, but most of the time when my mom has work to do she just stays at the office, and if my dad brings work home, he's always got a company laptop to do it on. I've got a computer in my room, so the only person who actually uses the office (as my mom insists on calling the room; the rest of us call it the den) is Cornelia, who does all her homework in it.

I stopped at the doorway and surveyed the room, my eyes lingering on the filing cabinet. My mom was always sticking stuff in there, but I didn't know what.

It's dangerous for you to be together.

Bennett, Henry.

Bennett, Cornelia.

Bennett, Katharine.

Bennett, Edmund.

It wasn't like I'd been told never to open the filing cabinet, but as I crossed the room, I found myself making up excuses to use for why I was there if my mom and my sister suddenly arrived home and found me snooping in the family files. *Do we have any blank paper anywhere? Is this where we keep the printer cartridges?*

Are you and Dad engaged in some kind of secret or illegal activity?

I grabbed the handle of the top drawer and pulled it slightly. The cabinet was old and wooden, but my mom hates drawers that stick, so after she'd bought it at some yard sale, she'd gotten all new works for it and the drawers slid easily on their ball bearings. I pulled it out as far as it would go and began thumbing through the files. *American Express. Cornelia, report cards. Katharine, business receipts. Cornelia, medical forms. Frequent flier stuff.* I shut the drawer and went to the next one. Used date books were piled high—both of my parents are pretty old school about stuff like calendars, and my mom likes to keep hers. She says it's for tax purposes, but I think it's because she likes when we're all arguing about whether the four of us went to dinner at Luigi's the night we went to see *The Lion King*, she can grab the appropriate book and announce with complete authority that we did.

I reached down and grabbed one from the pile. It was from 2006, and I flipped open to September 14. *1:30. Dr. Pinto.*

Dr. Pinto was our dentist. And at 1:30 on September 14, 2006, my mother had gone to see him.

Clearly, this was a woman who was hiding something.

My phone buzzed a text from Nia.

CHURCH/FAM DAY/ENG ESSAY. C U TMRW.

I slid the drawer shut, feeling a little dirty for having opened it in the first place. And what was I hoping to find, anyway? If my parents were hiding something, was it really going to be shoved in a drawer somewhere with Cornelia's old report cards? Didn't spies have safe deposit boxes? Safe houses?

I decided that my punishment for having invaded my parents' privacy would be that I'd stay home and not meet my mom and Cornelia, thereby depriving myself of a Rosie's Belgian waffle. I'd eat the muffin they brought me, though.

I mean, it wasn't like I'd found anything.

As I headed into the kitchen to grab some pre-muffin OJ, my phone buzzed a second text. Callie.

HUGE HISTORY TEST TMRW. C U @ REHEARSAL.

Strike two.

Should I call them? Tell them what Frieda had said? Or was it the kind of news you had to deliver in person?

As I wondered what to do, the warning bell Callie's and Nia's texts had rung in my brain began to toll louder—I'd gotten an extension on my bio lab, and I still hadn't written much more than a sentence for my history essay. Would my mom even let me *go* to rehearsal if my teachers started sending warning notes home? I gulped down my orange juice and headed upstairs. Homework may have just been another brick in the wall, but try telling my mom that.

An hour later, as I was finishing up my lab report, I heard the garage door open, then my mom calling my name as she headed upstairs. "Hal, you awake?" she called as she got to my room. She stopped at the threshold. "Hi, honey. How's it going?"

I kept my eyes on the page, sure if she looked into them, she'd know I'd been poking around in her stuff. "Fine."

"We brought you a muffin." I glanced over at where she stood. She was holding a white paper bag in front of her and she looked like she always did—medium-length hair up in a sloppy ponytail, sweatshirt, red jeans with a pair of bright green Converse sneakers. She smiled at me and nodded toward the bag. "Blueberry."

Why were you on Thornhill's list, Mom? Is there something about our lives that you're not telling me?

But to ask her that, I'd have to tell her how I knew she was on Thornhill's list. And it wasn't like my mom would be all, *I understand, Hal. If you don't want to tell me anything about why you were able to see a secret list of names on your vice principal's computer, that's okay. Even if this is the same vice principal who's now in a coma and being held at Orion General—wait, what's that you say? He's* not *at Orion General anymore? He's been moved to an undisclosed location? Well, that's certainly none of my business, but if you want to continue investigating these crimes, more power to you. I'll help you in any way I can.*

I shook my head to clear the silent conversation I was having with myself. "Thanks, Mom."

She stepped into my room, kissed me gently on the top of my head, and dropped the bag with the muffin in it onto my desk. "Sure, sweetheart." Then she reached down and gave me a quick hug. "Love you."

"Love you, too, Mom."

As I opened the bag, I realized those were the only honest words I'd spoken to my mother in weeks.

I slept like crap, and I must have looked at least as bad as I felt because at lunch Nia asked me if I was okay. I wanted to tell her about what had happened in Baltimore, but the lunchroom was packed and way too noisy for a whispered conversation to have been audible even to someone with senses as keen as hers.

"Fine," I snapped, irritated about having to wait.

"O-*kay*." She held up her hands as if to show there wasn't a weapon in either of them, then began opening the containers that held her food. One had an elaborate collection of vegetables, one held some kind of tomato-y sauce, and one was a packet of what I swear was homemade bread.

I looked down at my slightly crushed peanut-butter-and-jelly sandwich. "Our parents have *nothing* in common!"

Nia dipped a pepper into the sauce and took a bite. "Oh, I wouldn't say that." She considered them for a moment. "They're alive."

I rolled my eyes. "You're hilarious."

"They are," she insisted, shrugging. "And they're married."

"So, what, you think Thornhill's list is just people who are alive and married? And then a few random Orion teenagers thrown in for good measure?" Uttering the words "Thornhill's list" made me lose my appetite, and I pushed the tinfoil with my sandwich on it away from me.

"They all live in Orion," Nia continued calmly. "They're all college educated; they all have at least one child—"

"You're describing *thousands of people*!" I practically shouted. A guy I didn't know sitting at the next table looked over at us, and I glared at him until he looked away before muttering to myself, "I am so mad at Amanda for doing this to us."

"Were you guys a couple?"

"What?" I was so surprised by Nia's non sequitur I nearly fell off my chair. She was studying me across a fork that had a piece of green pepper laced delicately through the tines.

"What what?" Nia asked. "Amanda was hot, there's no denying that. And you're a guy. It's hardly the weirdest question to ask."

"You couldn't . . . go *out* with Amanda," I stuttered.

"*One* couldn't or *you* couldn't?" Nia popped the pepper into her mouth, still staring at me.

"Some girls are just . . ." I shook my head and opened my eyes wide, as if I'd just made a definitive point.

Unfortunately, I hadn't.

Nia continued to stare.

"Okay, you know how . . ." I began. Then I thought about it. What I wanted to tell her about was white-water rafting with my family years ago, the crazy rush of the fall down the chutes, the sickening, fantastic, intense way we spun out of control and seemed about to hit the enormous boulders that lined the river we were flying down.

That was what it was like to be with Amanda. Thrilling. Stomach dropping. It made you glad to be alive, but it also made you scared for your life.

How could you be on a ride like that and think about romance?

And then, the last few miles of that trip, the river widened and the rapids evaporated. I could lie back in my raft and look at the sky and see the bluish mountains way off in the distance. It was a hot summer's day, and the water shimmered in the sun and the air smelled thick and wonderful, and every once in a while we'd pass a bank of wildflowers so colorful and brilliant you couldn't believe they were real. Life felt perfect and peaceful; I wanted the afternoon to last forever.

The only other times I ever felt like that were when I was with Callie.

Was this information I really needed Nia Rivera to have? Being with Nia was like a day spent ice-skating on a frozen lake—bracing, fun, kind of exhilarating even, but proceed at your own risk.

As it became clear I wasn't going to finish my sentence, Nia shrugged. "I sense you're pleading the Fifth."

Girls talked to one another. I might have had mostly guy friends and a sister who's not exactly president of a sorority, but my mom spends about half her life on the phone. Callie and Nia didn't strike me as the kind of girls who'd describe themselves as BFF, but did I want to risk Nia's telling Callie that I had a thing for Amanda?

I forced myself to meet her gaze. "I did not like Amanda, Nia," I said. "Not like that."

She nodded in a way that made me think I'd made my point. "Got it," she said.

By the time school ended, I was so tired I could have curled up anywhere—even the floor of the lobby—and easily lost consciousness for about a month.

Apparently I looked as exhausted as I felt because the first thing Callie said when she saw me at rehearsal was, "Are you sick, Hal?" She started to lift her hand, and for a second I thought she was going to check my forehead like my mom does when she wants to know if I have a fever. The thought of Callie's warm hand against my skin was so nice I almost forgot that I was supposed to be keeping her safe by keeping her away from me.

Nia was looking at her script and counting something; she didn't seem to hear Callie's question, instead announcing, "Twenty-five," as she slammed the play shut. "Tell Hal that on opening night, while he's enjoying the play from the audience, we will, between us, have twenty-five costume changes to oversee." She turned to me, eyes blazing, and her familiar glare was oddly friendly. It made me think of Frieda's warning. *When you're together you're . . .* I had no idea what she would have said if she'd been given the time to finish her sentence, but I know how I would have ended it.

When you're together you're happy.

From the stage, Mrs. Hayworth rallied her troops. "I need my costume crew."

I had to tell them about what Frieda had said. "Hey, guys . . ."

"*Now!*" Mrs. Hayworth bellowed.

Nia groaned. "That woman is the devil."

Callie shot me a questioning look, and I shrugged. I'd been waiting since Saturday; I could wait another couple of hours.

"It's cool. I'll tell you later. Meanwhile, any chance you've got something in there that I could take a look at, little lady?" I indicated her bag. On Friday afternoon I'd painted the final leaf on the final tree in an Arden that now looked remotely like a forest. Callie and Nia might be busier than ever with costume crew, but I had before me at least an hour or two of leisure.

Callie nodded and swung the pack off her shoulder. The way she handed it to me made me think it wasn't going to be all that heavy, but the momentum of her swing must have been greater than I realized because as I grabbed the strap of her bag, I almost dropped it.

"Whoa, this thing's heavy."

Callie shook her head and smiled a puzzled smile. "It's weird, sometimes it feels really heavy to me and sometimes it doesn't seem so bad." She shrugged. "I think it depends on how tired I am."

Well, after two sleepless nights, I was definitely tired. I made my way over to a seat toward the rear of the center section of the auditorium while Nia and Callie headed to the stage, Nia muttering something about people "who got volunteered for actual work while the people who volunteer them seem to end up having an enormous amount of free time on their hands." The word *time* made me think of Amanda's watch, its mysterious inscription, my own failure to figure out what she was trying to tell me.

Oh, yeah, Bennett. You're definitely *the man to unlock the mystery of this box.*

Since Louise's, I hadn't seen the box outside of the photographs Callie had taken and sent me and Nia, but it was just light enough in the auditorium for me to make out the carvings Callie had been trying to describe to us. I'd hoped getting my hands on the actual box would make it obvious to me that there were drawings like the ones Callie thought she'd seen, but the maze of vines and leaves was so intricate, it was hard to see if there were individual figures hidden in the carvings.

As I studied the pattern in search of hidden pictures, I was reminded of the summer before sixth grade, when I first moved to Orion and Callie and her mom took me stargazing. They tried to show me how to find the constellations, but I kept getting confused, thinking they meant one star when they meant another, connecting stars that weren't meant to be connected into shapes that seemed as clear as the ones they were trying to weave together for me. Ultimately I'd concluded that the constellations were about as scientific as alchemy, which had made Callie's mom laugh instead of making her angry.

"O, ye of little faith," she'd said, and as I remembered her saying that and thought of how brave Callie had been in the face of her mom's disappearing and her dad's losing it there for a while, I wanted to have faith, lots of faith, tons of faith. I wanted there to be not just drawings of animals but a map, a treasure map. A treasure map that pointed all the way to—

"Well, hello, stranger."

I jerked my head up.

And there, sitting in the seat next to mine, was none other than Heidi Bragg.

A lot of really strange things had happened to me over the past couple of weeks, but Heidi Bragg coming over to talk to me was without a doubt one of the strangest.

I didn't say anything. All I could think of were the horrible insults she'd hurled at Callie, the story Nia had told me about the I-Girls playing a mean trick on her in sixth grade, and the image of Heidi running down Bea Rossiter with her daddy's car.

My mom says it's wrong to hate anyone but Hitler, Pol Pot, Idi Amin, and George W. Bush. I couldn't help thinking that if she knew her better, she'd add Heidi Bragg to the list.

Heidi was wearing a low-cut pink T-shirt that showed why the guys in my grade liked her. She put her feet up on the chair in front of hers and went on talking like there was nothing the least bit unusual about our sitting and chatting. "So, what's up?"

"What do you want, Heidi?" My voice was sharp.

"Jeez, friendly much?" Raising her arms above her head, she gave a loud yawn, then looked back at me and nodded toward the box. "That's nice. Is it yours?"

For a brief second, I got the strangest sensation that she knew the answer to the question before she asked it. But then I realized I was being paranoid. Whoever "they" were, Dr. Joy was not being held hostage by a coven of fourteen-year-old, lip-glossed females who'd christened themselves with the brazenly stupid name of "I-Girls."

"Nope."

"So whose is it?" Heidi gave me a shy smile, like my "nope" was a flirtatious joke I was playing on her.

"It's Callie's, actually." I'd meant Callie's name to be a shot across the bow, an announcement about whose side I was on in the all-out social war that Heidi had declared. I almost wanted Heidi to say something mean about Callie just so I could . . . well, dumb as it may sound, I was ready to defend her honor and even her life, like Spiderman saving Mary Jane.

But to my amazement, instead of curling her lip in disgust or spitting out more invective against her former friend, Heidi just sighed.

"God, Callie must *totally* hate me." She turned away from me slightly, like she didn't want me to see how upset she was. "I bet she won't even show at the cast party since it's at my house."

I wasn't sure how to respond. Was Heidi seriously *surprised* that Callie hated her?

The box was heavy so I turned and put it on the seat next to me, then turned back to Heidi. "You can't be serious."

Heidi was staring straight ahead at the stage, where Ms. Garner was directing some of the crew to place a small mound of what was probably supposed to be dirt but actually resembled a pile of another brown substance.

"Don't you get it, Hal?" She shook her head and lowered her voice so I had to lean toward her. I was surprised by how good she smelled—not like Callie smelled good, but like the magazines filled with photos of well-dressed, skinny women on rooftops in New York that my dentist has in his waiting room.

I realized I'd half expected her to smell of sulfuric acid.

"Get what, Heidi?"

She sighed, as if the memory she was about to share was so painful it was hard for her to articulate it. "Callie and I were friends for a long time. You know, we *became* the I-Girls together and that was . . ." She looked up at the ceiling for a minute before turning back to me. "That was almost three years ago."

"What's your *point,* Heidi?"

Leaning against the armrest on the other side of her seat from me, she wound her hair around her index finger. I watched as her finger twirled around and around. "Can't you see, Hal? She betrayed me."

I couldn't believe what I was hearing. "*She* betrayed *you*? Heidi, you said she was dead to you. And I think you called us 'freakazoid weirdos' in front of half the school."

Heidi shook her head at the memory. "What Callie did was really painful, Hal." She swallowed. "I'm not proud of how I acted, but haven't *you* ever done anything *you're* ashamed of?"

In spite of myself, I thought of my solo trip to Baltimore. It wasn't exactly behavior of the month.

"I don't know what to say," I said honestly. Was it possible we'd . . . been wrong about Heidi? I remembered how much Nia had hated Callie at first, but how over time she'd come to trust and believe in her.

Could something like that happen with Heidi Bragg?

Heidi snickered a little. "You know, Hal, I sometimes wonder . . ."

"What?" I asked, curious.

And suddenly Heidi's giggles became laughter so loud some people sitting a few rows ahead of us turned to see what the joke was. Confused, I watched her get to her feet.

"What do I *wonder,* Hal?" And the sad, hurt girl who'd sat

beside me a moment earlier was gone. In her place was the terrifying creature I'd always thought of when I thought of Heidi Bragg. "I'll tell you. I *wonder* how someone who's as naive as you manages to survive. That's what I *wonder*." And with that, she turned and strode down the row and along the center aisle to the front of the auditorium where most of the cast was gathered.

Okay, that was completely bizarre.

Did I imagine that entire random exchange? I looked at the seat she'd vacated, but if she'd been an apparition, she didn't suddenly reappear. Her coming over to talk to and then insult me was just so odd, so . . . purposeless. So . . .

And suddenly I felt sick. Had Heidi's descending on me really been purposeless? Or had it had a very, very specific motive? Even before I turned my head to my left I was pretty sure what I'd find—or what I *wouldn't* find.

Sure enough, my eyes, when they landed on the seat that only a few minutes earlier had held Amanda's box, only confirmed what I already knew.

The seat was empty.

The box was gone.

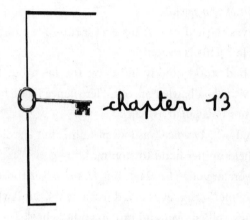

chapter 13

"Well, what did you *think* she was coming over for?"

"I just thought—" Confronted by Nia's fury, I found it nearly impossible to form a sentence. I was used to calming Nia down, yes, but because she was mad at *other* people. Nia mad at you and in your face was a way, way scarier experience than just Nia mad.

"Ooh, let me guess!" She waved her hands over an imaginary crystal ball. "It's coming to me. Yes, you had a feeling! And your feeling told you that letting Heidi Bragg have Amanda's most precious, most treasured—"

"I screwed *up*, okay, Nia?" I'd already told them of my frantic search up and down the aisles and my panicked, fruitless hunt backstage for the box or Heidi herself. "Haven't *you* ever screwed up?" To my horror I realized my question almost parroted Heidi's earlier one to me.

Haven't you ever done anything you're ashamed of, Hal?

Well, yes, Heidi, as a matter of fact, I have—I believed something that came out of your mouth.

Nia's eyes flashed fire. "This isn't a run-of-the-mill screw-up, okay, Hal? This is *colossal*."

Callie had stood quietly by us on the lawn out front of Endeavor while Nia bawled me out. Her silence made me think she might not be as mad as Nia.

"Callie, I—" My voice was low, pleading, but she shook her head and held up her hand to stop me.

"If it were anyone else, Hal. But *Heidi*? After those things she said to me?" Her eyes filled with tears, and when she blinked, they spilled over and ran down her cheeks.

I thought of the night on Crab Apple Hill when she'd told us what had happened with Beatrice Rossiter, how she'd let me wipe away her tears after she cried.

Now I wasn't the one comforting her, I was the one making her cry.

Maybe embarrassed by her tears, Callie suddenly said, "I've gotta go," and dashed for her bike. Nia and I watched her leave, but there was no solidarity in our standing together. Callie's hands must have been shaking because it took her a long time to get her bike unlocked. Once she did, she just jumped on and pedaled off, not turning around to wave good-bye.

As soon as she was gone, Nia turned to me. "Just so we're clear, you *do* realize you basically handed Amanda's most treasured possession to her enemy."

And even though (or maybe *because*) Nia's words only

stated what I already knew, I felt the need to defend myself. "Oh, get off your high horse, Nia. You don't know that that box was any more important to Amanda than any other item in Louise's store."

"Except Louise didn't tell us it would be very, very dangerous for the wrong people to get ahold of her snakeskin clutch." Nia gave a bitter laugh before pointing an accusing finger at me. "Keep telling yourself it's not a big deal, Hal. Maybe that'll make it true."

"She doesn't even know the box belongs to Amanda," I pointed out, desperate. "Maybe it was only . . . maybe she just wanted to show she *could* take it."

Nia crossed her arms and stared at me, her voice sickeningly sweet and faux-reassuring. "You're right, Hal. We don't know why she wanted it. Maybe because she thought Callie would miss it and she wanted to hurt her. Maybe she just *liked* it." As if she'd flipped a switch, her tone changed and became accusatory. "Is that your defense, Hal? That we don't have to worry about Heidi's having Amanda's box because we don't know why she wanted it?"

"I . . ." God, how did Nia always manage to make me sound like *such* a total jackass?

As I stood there, mouth practically hanging open with inarticulation, she walked over to her bike, unlocked it, and headed out of the parking lot.

"Thanks for your understanding!" I shouted after her lamely, but she was too far off (in every way) to respond.

As I watched Nia disappear into the darkening evening,

the truth of her words hit me full force in a way it couldn't when I was so focused on deflecting her anger.

You basically handed Amanda's most treasured possession to her enemy.

I'd lost it. Me. I'd practically . . . given it away. For all we knew, the box had a map directing us to where we could find her. Or maybe there were letters inside it explaining why she'd had to disappear. At the very least, it held items that she valued, things she'd wanted kept safe, not just because someone was after her and could take them, but because they were hers.

"'S elf-trust is the first secret of success,'" Amanda said. "What?"

We were sitting on the train coming home from Baltimore, and I was basking in the afterglow of the most perfect day of my life. Frieda and I had really talked about art, arguing about John Currin (me: he's a fraud; Frieda: he's a genius) and public funding for the arts, the power of oils versus the pleasure of watercolors, the need to show your work versus the desire to keep it private. Her loft, which was also her studio, was full of pieces in progress as well as ones she had finished, quick sketches I took to be studies for future projects, photos pulled from magazines and tacked up on the bulletin board that covered one entire wall. The floor had, no doubt, been a pristine white at some point, but by now there was so much paint spattered under our feet that looking down felt almost as much like looking at a painting as did looking at the actual canvases hung all around us. There were three enormous skylights open to the brilliant blue sky, and one wall of the studio was all windows, so there seemed to be nothing standing between us and the rooftops. Talking to Frieda made me realize I had opinions on things I'd never thought I cared about, and I found myself imagining living in just such a loft someday, maybe in New York or Rome or hey, what the hell, even Baltimore.

For the first time in my life, I could see what it would be like to live the life of an artist.

Amanda repeated herself. "I said, 'Self-trust is the first secret of success.'" Even though we'd left home early that morning and walked in a brisk breeze for at least a mile along the river before standing in the windblown harbor to admire the waterfront, Amanda's hair was still in its perfect, tight bun, as coiffed and polished as if she'd borrowed not just the clothing but the spirit of the 1950s office girl she was impersonating for the day.

"Oh," I said as she looked at me over a pair of glasses attached to a chain around her neck—glasses I was about ninety percent sure she didn't need. (Ninety was about the highest percentage of definite I ever felt when it came to Amanda.)

The train's gentle rocking was having a lulling effect—I wanted to close my eyes and slip into half dreams about a future in a sunny loft with a paint-covered floor and an Italian espresso machine like the one Frieda had used to make us coffee far too bitter for a wimp like me to drink.

"Do you trust yourself, Hal?"

Did I trust myself? Could I trust myself, believe in myself, enough to follow my dream of devoting my life to art?

I wasn't sure.

The look she gave was so intense, so searching, I almost

couldn't hold her stare. "Because I trust you, Hal."

She waited a beat, completely comfortable with our staring at each other. Then, the second before I had to look away, she took my hand gently in hers. "I trust you completely, Hal."

"Well, thanks," I said. "I appreciate your trusting me, Valentino." I was half joking, half serious when I added, "But you should probably put me to the test, you know? See if I'm worthy."

Amanda took off her glasses, leaned her head back against the seat, and smiled what I had come to think of as her Mona Lisa smile. "Oh, I will, Hal Bennett. I will."

She'd been telling the truth that day. She had put me to the test.

And I'd failed.

I thought I'd gotten used to my dad traveling all the time, but when I stepped into the house and saw his bag sitting by the doorway, the sense of relief that washed over me made me realize just how much I'd missed him while he was gone.

"Dad?"

"Kitchen." The house smelled amazing, so his answer was no surprise.

I followed the mouthwatering scent of garlic browning in olive oil to where my dad was standing at the counter, chopping something green and leafy. My mom and my sister and I always tease him for being totally OCD when it comes to cooking—his recipes inevitably involve dicing about ten thousand vegetables into tiny pieces and placing them very carefully into piles that he adds to a sauce over the course of about forty-eight hours. He says he's not compulsive, that cooking is all about precision. My mom says he should be more relaxed about food preparation, like she is, but Cornelia and I have eaten food she's cooked, and if you want my honest opinion, when it comes to the kitchen, my mom should relax a little less.

"When'd you get home?" I pulled out the stool by the counter and plopped down to watch him cook. When he was a teenager, he spent his summers as a line cook, so my dad can dice and slice like one of those guys selling knives on infomercials. Watching him is completely hypnotic.

"About an hour ago. How's it going?"

"Um . . ." How, exactly, was I supposed to answer him? *Well, my friend disappeared and my other friends and I are trying to find her and we have reason to believe that she's being pursued by evil people who want to seriously hurt her.*

What I finally settled on didn't exactly cut to the heart of the matter. "Okay, I guess." There was an open bag of chips on the counter and I took a handful.

"Okay?" my dad repeated. He didn't slow his chopping, but something about his inflection gave me the sense he knew there was more to the story.

I swallowed my last chip and took another. My dad let the silence between us grow, but I couldn't tell if he was trying to make me uncomfortable enough to spill everything or if he didn't mind the quiet. Like I said before, my dad's not exactly the most social being on the planet.

Finally, I had to say something. "Amanda's still missing."

He nodded and swept a handful of olives off the chopping board and into a bowl to his right, then reached behind himself to turn off the burner under the saucepan with the olive oil and garlic on it. *Graceful* isn't a word I'd normally use to describe a guy, but it perfectly captures my dad in the kitchen.

"Yes, Mom told me." He wiped off the cutting board and dropped a tomato onto it, starting to cut it into squares almost before it hit the wood.

"What else did Mom say?" My mom was never what you'd call a big Amanda fan. In fact, I think she might have *almost* hated her. My mom's not exactly square, but her idea of letting it all hang out is casual Friday. She definitely didn't find Amanda's changes of clothes and personas charming; she found them disturbing and she thought Amanda was bad news. When she heard Amanda had disappeared, she said, "I'm so sorry that friend of yours went missing; I hope they find her." What she meant was, *I hope they find her and put her in an institution for troubled teens, which is so obviously where she belongs.*

Maybe because the answer would have been unrepeatable, my dad didn't respond to my question. Instead, he said, "It's worrying."

"I know!" I hadn't meant to shout, but it was such a relief to have someone, an adult, think what I thought about Amanda's disappearance. Not that it was crazy or criminal but that it was something that should elicit worry.

My mom would have jumped on my outburst (*Why are you worried? Do you know something you're not telling me?*), but my dad just said, "I want you to be careful." He paused, put his knife down, and looked at me for a long beat before adding, "Be very, very careful, Hal."

Was it my imagination or were we talking about something more than Amanda's disappearance, more than the attack on Mr. Thornhill?

"Dad?" I asked. My voice was a near-whisper. "Dad, do you . . . know something?"

My dad whisked the diced tomato into a bowl and grabbed for another one. He held it for a long minute, studying the bright red fruit as if it held the answer to an important question. Then he looked at me. "I know some *things*." He emphasized the difference between my question and his answer.

Okay, I couldn't tell my mom about Thornhill's list, but could I tell my dad? Or would he automatically tell Mom?

My dad started chopping his tomato, then stopped. Still looking down at the cutting board, his voice tight, he said, "If I could protect you from every bad thing in the world, I would do that. You know that, right?" He raised his eyes to look at me, and to my amazement, I saw that he was tearing up.

I nodded, too shocked to speak. This was so not like my dad. My mom can start bawling over the idea of me and Cornelia dying of old age someday. But my *dad*? My dad practically crying about our safety?

Something was *definitely* going on.

He coughed softly. When he continued, his voice was normal and I wondered if I'd imagined he'd been upset at all. "Well, you're definitely dealing with a lot. One friend missing, new friends on the scene. I always liked Callie.

And I've heard good things about Nia."

Wait, how had we gotten here? He'd been about to tell me something, I was sure of it.

"Dad?" I began.

"Dad, are you still chopping?" It was Cornelia. She came into the kitchen and stood next to my stool.

"Hey!" My dad turned to look at her and said, "Sure you don't want to help me cook?"

Was it my imagination, or was he purposely avoiding looking at me?

"Pass, Dad. Hal, can I talk to you for a second?" Cornelia's voice was urgent. Or at least as urgent as Cornelia's voice gets. My heart skipped a beat. Had she found something? Had she found *someone*? Suddenly I was just as interested in what my sister knew as in what my dad did. Still, I hesitated. Cornelia was always around. Lately, my dad never was.

"Better see what she wants," my dad said. It sounded just enough like an order that I got to my feet. Trying to talk to my dad if he doesn't want to talk is a lost cause. "We'll eat when your mom gets home," he called after our retreating backs. A second later I heard him switch on NPR.

"Cornelia, do you ever wonder about Dad's job?" I asked as we walked through the dining room.

"He's a consultant for Market Partners Consolidated International. They specialize in coordinating consolidations for international companies that—"

God, she sounded like one of the brochures he sometimes left lying around. "I know what he *does*," I said, impatient.

"Officially. I'm just wondering if . . . if he does something else, too."

"Yes," said Cornelia.

"Yes?" I snapped my head around to stare at her. "Yes he does something else?"

Cornelia's voice was calm. "Yes, I wonder about it, too."

"Do you—"

She cut me off. "What I'm about to show you is of a time-sensitive nature. Do you want to see it or not?"

Time-sensitive nature sounded serious. Of course, so was the possibility of our dad's having some kind of secret life. "What is it?"

"I want to talk to you about Thornhill's computer."

Thornhill's computer. Could she get me access to his files? Because if she could, maybe my screwup with Nia and Callie didn't have to be permanent. Maybe if I went to them with the infamous list, they'd forgive me for losing Amanda's box. Maybe everything between us would be the way it was before I basically handed Heidi Bragg all of Amanda's most precious secrets.

"What? What about Thornhill's computer? Did you find a way to get onto it?" Without realizing what I was doing, I practically lunged at her.

Something about my hysteria (or perhaps it was my rabid tone of voice) made her stare at me intently with those assessing eyes of hers. She held her hand up to indicate I should take a step back toward something resembling sanity.

I did.

"Are you seriously going to do something to his Facebook account?"

"What?" I remembered our first conversation about it. "No. Cornelia, I was joking. I thought you knew that."

"Why would I know that?"

Sometimes Cornelia could be so literal it drove me crazy. "Cornelia, we're in the middle of a major crisis. Our friend is missing. Mr. Thornhill is in a coma and he may have been kidnapped. Do you really think I would take time out to play a practical joke on a man who's lying somewhere in a hospital bed *unconscious*?"

Cornelia shrugged. "Well, why did you take time out to joke with me?"

"Cornelia!" I yanked on my hair to keep from screaming.

She was unmoved by my dramatic display of frustration. "We don't really have time for you to freak out." She glanced at her watch. "Mom's going to be home soon." I knew what she meant—my dad's not exactly a follow-your-kids-around-and-see-what-they're-doing kind of parent, but as soon as my mom gets home from work she always comes to find us and say hello and see how our homework is going, etc.

In short, Dad's being around wasn't a problem, but if we had any . . . questionable activities, we definitely wanted to engage in them while our mother was safely out of the house.

Cornelia turned and continued on toward the den. Just seeing the filing cabinet where I'd fruitlessly searched for clues made me embarrassed.

She dropped into the rolling desk chair and gestured for

me to sit on the sofa. Behind her, the screen saver showed insanely bright tropical fish swimming happy and oblivious through a digital salty paradise.

"What do you know about unilateral computer networks?" she asked.

"Um, nothing?" I offered.

Cornelia paused for a second, like a person translating a speech in her head from one language to another. Then she began to talk. "Okay, with most computer networks, information can flow in both directions." Cornelia made her hands into fists and held them shoulder-width apart. "I can enter information on this computer"—she wiggled her right fist— "and retrieve it on this one"—she wiggled her left fist. "Or I can enter information on *this* computer"—she wiggled her left fist—"and retrieve it on *this* one"—she wiggled her right one.

"I'm actually following this." I settled into a comfortable position. One of the coolest things about Cornelia is how she can make you think you understand how computers work.

"A unilateral computer network is different," Cornelia continued after a brief nod to acknowledge my announcement that I am not completely dim-witted. "In a unilateral computer network, information can only travel one way."

"Uni!" I shouted. "One."

She ignored my enthusiasm. "Yes, uni indicates a single direction, and a unilateral network is a basic way of protecting a central database that people will be accessing from remote locations."

Her last sentence made me slightly less confident than I

had been a moment ago. "Okay, you're *kind of* losing me now."

Sighing, Cornelia made her explanation even simpler. "Say you're a business and you want your employees to be able to work at home and send their work to a central computer in the building to be printed. But you *don't* want your competition to be able to hack into your mainframe and download your new secret recipe for the world's greatest chocolate chip cookie." Again, she held her fists apart. "Employee X goes home, types up his PowerPoint presentation *here*, emails it to the design people *here* to be made into booklets for tomorrow's meeting." She moved one of her fists on each "here." "But when Competitor Y wants to sneak into your network and get the cookie recipe, he can't do it because information can only *enter* the system, not leave it."

"Got it."

"Some unilateral networks go the other way. You might want your employees to be able to take information from a central network without being able to download anything *to* that network, like a virus. Either way, a unilateral system is the first line of defense in a lot of computer networks. Even the CIA and NSA start by creating unilateral systems and build from there."

"Wait, you know about the CIA's and NSA's computer systems?"

Cornelia stared at me but didn't say anything.

"Sorry," I said finally, and she continued.

"Endeavor has a unilateral computer network."

Incredibly enough, I'd gotten so caught up in Cornelia's

explanation of unilateral computer networks that I'd actually forgotten there was a point. When she said the word *Endeavor*, however, it all came rushing back at me.

"Okay," I said, my voice as even as I could make it.

"That means that teachers can enter grades into the system from home, but they couldn't download a kid's permanent record, for instance."

"Okay," I repeated.

"There's one exception."

I felt my throat grow dry. Instead of trying to speak, I just nodded.

"One user has switched the direction of the unilateral system."

I licked my lips with my suddenly parched tongue. "You're saying there's one computer that can take information *out* of Endeavor's central computer."

"And that Endeavor's central computer cannot access," she added, nodding.

"And that computer belongs to—" I began.

"Mr. Thornhill," we finished together.

There was a pause as we allowed what she'd discovered to sink in.

"It's actually not that complicated, what he did," Cornelia went on. "He basically replaced, or I should say supplemented, the open unilateral system of the network with a closed, reverse unilateral system between his computer and the school's mainframe." My head was spinning so fast I missed some of what she said. Something about his computer being an unspecified "hub" with the ability to engage in "data interfacing" with a computer from a remote location.

"The point," she finished, either because she was done or because she could tell she'd lost me a few miles back, "is that the school recognizes something different about Mr. Thornhill's computer and will release information to it."

"So you're saying if we can get Mr. Thornhill's laptop, we can get the data he was downloading." For the first time ever, I was a little disappointed in Cornelia. I mean, you didn't have to be a computer genius to know that if we *had* Thornhill's computer we could have the *information* on it.

"I'm saying the school computer will release information to any computer it thinks is Mr. Thornhill's," Cornelia corrected, and though it took me a second to realize what she was saying, when I finally did, I literally leaped to my feet.

"So if the school's mainframe thought, say, this"—I pointed at the computer on the desk behind Cornelia—"was Thornhill's computer . . ."

"Then it would send or resend to it any documents it was asked to produce." And with that, Cornelia spun around and hit a button on the keyboard.

An instant later, I was looking at a familiar computer screen, one I had seen less than a week earlier in the vice principal's office.

One I had thought I would never be able to see again.

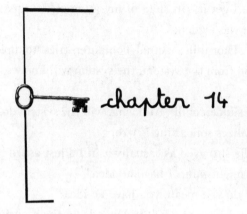

chapter 14

"There's a catch," Cornelia said from the chair beside me.

Michael Zalin . . . the name meant nothing to me. *Zoe Costas* . . . definitely a kid in our grade. *Samara Cole* . . . no idea. The list wasn't alphabetical, and I just skimmed it hoping for a familiar name. *Beatrice Rossiter* was there. *Frieda Levinson*. Aha. Some of the names had little paper clip icons next to them; some didn't. I scrolled down the page. There I was: *Henry Bennett*. As I went to click on the icon, Cornelia touched the back of my hand to get my attention.

"I said, there's a catch," and her tone made it clear she wanted a hundred percent of my attention.

"Sorry. I'm listening." I made myself turn away from the screen and meet her level gaze.

"The central computer at Endeavor thinks this"—

she pointed at the screen in front of us—"is Thornhill's computer."

"Right, I got it." In spite of my attempts to squash it, my impatience was evident.

"So if Thornhill's actual computer tries to upload any information from the system, the system will know something is wrong."

I felt a sudden chill. "And what will the system do, exactly, when it realizes something is wrong?"

Cornelia shrugged as casually as if I'd just asked her if she thought it might rain. "I have no idea."

"What do you mean, you have no idea?"

"I mean I have no idea. It depends on the security he put in place. Maybe he's set it up so he can simultaneously log on from two computers."

"Oh," I said, relieved. "Cool."

My relief was short-lived.

"Or maybe," she offered, "as soon as his computer logs on the system will send a virus to *both* 'Thornhill' computers and destroy them."

I thought of all the places Thornhill's computer could be. His office, possibly. The police station. With Dr. Joy. Or Frieda's mysterious "*they*."

"It gets more complicated," Cornelia continued.

"I'm so wishing we weren't having this conversation."

"It's possible that the connection between Thornhill's system and the Endeavor system has a GPS component."

I was completely confused. "GPS? You mean the thing in

Mom's car that she's always saying gives bad directions?"

"I mean that thing in Mom's car that tells you where you are."

"O-kaaay," I said slowly. "So that would mean . . . ?"

"That would mean if someone knows about the system Thornhill set up, or if someone found *out* about the system, that person could track Thornhill's computer using GPS."

I thought about what Cornelia was saying, then pointed at our mother's computer. "That person would be able to track this computer."

"Right," said Cornelia.

"That person would be able to find the physical location of this computer."

"Right," Cornelia repeated.

"That person—" I began, but this time she cut me off.

"I think," she said, "that you should find what you're looking for as quickly as possible and then shut down the computer."

"Once I do that, will we be able to get back on?"

Cornelia shrugged. "We might. Like I said, it depends on the security Thornhill set up."

"So you're saying I need to find what I'm looking for fast and I might never be able to access this information again," I summarized.

"That," said Cornelia, standing up, "is exactly what I'm saying."

In dreams, I'm sometimes trying to dial a phone or unlock a door but my hands are shaking so badly I can't hit the right numbers or I keep dropping my key ring before I can get the key in the lock. Sitting at my mother's computer and trying to make my way around Thornhill's files as quickly as possible, I felt like I was in one of those dreams. I went to hit the paper clip icon next to my name and ended up hitting an entry two names down: Sol Rosa. The screen immediately filled with photos of someone I'd never met, but when I went to go back, I didn't move the curser up high enough and I ended up opening one of the folders in Sol Rosa's file. Suddenly I was looking at a scan of a third-grade transcript, where I learned Sol "has done impressive work mastering cursive." I clicked back, found my name again, and hit the right paper clip this time.

But what I found was almost as bewildering as what I'd left. At least a dozen photos of me appeared on the screen. The first was from a road trip my parents and I had taken cross-country the summer before Cornelia was born (my mom was pregnant with her at the time). I was standing between them in front of a sign that said ELEVATION 12,671 FEET. In the background were mountaintops so high they disappeared into the mist. I was giving the photographer a thumbs-up, and both my parents were smiling for the camera. I had no recollection of the trip and no idea where we were at the moment the photo was snapped.

In the next picture, I was with my dad and we were sitting in a boat, fishing. Neither of us was looking at the camera; it was like we didn't even realize we were being photographed. I looked at the next photo: a shot of me breaking a ribbon at a race I'd run in seventh grade—an Orion Township 10K—something I'd entered before I joined the track team in eighth grade.

My heart pounded in my chest. What the hell was going on? Why did Thornhill have all these pictures of me? It was almost like . . . had he been *following* me for some reason?

I clicked away from the screen with the photos to a document called L-C33159, and there was a list of addresses, places my family had lived. It was brief—both of our houses in Philly followed by our address in Orion. I clicked to a new file and found myself staring at the Bennett family tree.

There were tons of other documents. Report cards, medical records, IQ tests. Even vision and hearing tests that I had no memory of taking. I clicked back to the main list and clicked on Cornelia. Again there were the photos, the addresses, the school records. Seeing so much intimate information about my family members was starting to make me sick. Something dripped onto the keyboard, and I realized I was sweating. Wiping at my forehead with the back of my hand, I clicked away from Cornelia and onto a stranger, Maude Cooper. Maude was a short, older woman, maybe fifty. There was a photo of her standing in front of a house with a guy who might have been her husband. Maude, too, lived in Orion, as did Stefanie Stone and Laden Chapel. Back at the main list, I clicked on Beatrice Rossiter.

I'd forgotten how pretty Beatrice had been before the accident. There was a picture of her standing with her mom (a tall, gorgeous African American woman) and her dad (a way-shorter and skinny white man with enormous glasses) in front of a restaurant that looked like it was in some European city.

I clicked on a folder marked PC13342+13367 and suddenly the screen was filled almost entirely with a black-and-white picture of two smiling girls in identical wigs.

The girls looked so much alike that for a second I found myself thinking, *I didn't know Beatrice had a sister,* and then I gasped. Because the smiling girl next to Beatrice wasn't some unknown sister I'd never met.

It was Amanda.

"Hi, guys, I'm home!"

I'd been sure I'd hear the garage door open, that I'd have time to exit whatever file I was looking at and pull up some innocuous blank Word document, but clearly I'd been wrong. I heard my dad talking, then my mother was calling, "Hal! Hal, come say hello."

Beatrice and Amanda were friends?! I'd never seen them together and she'd never once mentioned her to me.

Not exactly a shocker, though, right?

"Hal? Are you upstairs?"

"Um, coming, Mom!" Beatrice and Amanda. Did Callie and Nia know? Nah. Callie had told us every detail of the night of Beatrice's accident; there was no way she would have left out the fact that Amanda wanted her to do right by Beatrice because they were friends.

"Hal?"

My mom's voice was coming from just beyond the den. If she came in and found me looking at a photo of Amanda, she'd start asking questions. *Lots* of questions. I clicked out of the window and onto my name, then spun around to face the door, hoping my expression wouldn't betray just how totally I was freaking out.

But just as I put my feet down to stop my spin, I realized what a colossal error I'd made in clicking back on my own file. The pictures of our family were guaranteed to catch my mom's eye, make her come over to see what I was working on. I needed to . . . I needed to . . .

"There you are!" She appeared in the doorway, still wearing her bright red raincoat and yellow hat.

It was too late. My mom was smiling at me, her eyes bright with pleasure at everyone's being home. I waited for them to widen when she saw what was on the screen behind me, but all she did was nod when I said hello.

"Dad's home!" she announced with enthusiasm.

What do you say when your parent states the obvious yet you do not want to piss her off? "Yes!" I half shouted, trying to match her excitement. Had she not seen the screen? Had she been too distracted by the prospect of a rare family dinner (one she did not have to cook) to focus on the pictures? Or maybe . . . of course, the screen saver must have come back on. She wasn't looking at the computer screen because she didn't care about a bunch of random tropical fish.

My mom pulled off her hat. "Good day?"

"Oh, yeah!" My relief translated itself into enthusiasm and I actually clapped my hands together.

"That's great, sweetie." She came over and kissed the top of my head, then headed back toward the kitchen. "Dad says dinner is in about thirty minutes."

I touched my hand to my damp forehead and breathed deeply in, then out. What I needed was to calm down. What I needed was a system. I'd look at the files of people I knew and compare them to the files of strangers. What did Hal Bennett have in common with Maude Cooper? What did Callista Leary have in common with Stefanie Stone? I reached into the middle desk drawer, took out a pad with Orion Community College printed on it, and grabbed a pencil from the Orioles mug on the desktop. Then I turned around and prepared to get to work.

But instead of facing a screen full of tropical fish, I faced a screen full of . . . nothing. No fish. No photos of me. Just darkness. I hit the Space key, then the Enter key, but still there was no response. I listened and realized that not only was the screen dead, but the computer itself was off.

Heart pounding, I pushed the Power button.

Nothing.

I pushed it again, this time holding it for a count of five. I released it, counted to thirty, then pushed it again.

Nothing.

There was no doubt about it: Something—or someone—had just murdered my computer.

Don't you know it's dangerous for you to be together?

They've got him.

You gave Amanda's most treasured possession to her enemy.

I put my head down on the cool plastic of the keyboard and tried to convince myself everything was going to be okay.

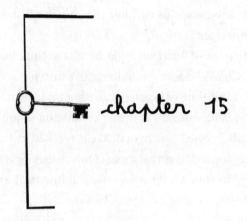

chapter 15

As the week passed, I realized I was slipping back into my pre-Amanda, pre–Callie and Nia life, as if being friends with them was a summer vacation that had come to an end. I ran into Charlie, the drummer for Girl Like Me, in the hall on Friday at lunch, and he slapped me on the back and said, "Where have you been, man?"

I didn't know what to tell him. *I've been with my friends?* But were Callie and Nia even my friends anymore? *I've been with my fellow guides.*

Sure, Hal. Hare Krishna much?

I ended up just shrugging. "Around."

Somehow I was walking with him toward the cafeteria as he talked. "Dude, you missed the worst practice last week. Brian's mom was all, 'You're too loud,' and Brian's all, 'It's a band, Mom,' and she's all, 'Well, be a quieter band.'" He shook his head with amazement at Brian's mom's failure to appreciate classic rock. "She made us turn off the amp. It's like we're Girl Like Me unplugged."

I couldn't really focus on what he was saying, but luckily talking to Charlie doesn't require active listening. The guy could have a fulfilling conversation with a tablecloth.

"Yeah," I said, not sure if it was a total non sequitur.

"Seriously messed up, right?" We'd reached the cafeteria and Charlie crossed the threshold. Only when he'd actually been talking to thin air for a few steps did he turn around to see where I was.

"You eating?"

It was just after noon, and the cafeteria was filling up. I looked around, but neither Callie nor Nia was there. Simultaneously relieved and disappointed, I just shook my head. "Nah, I've gotta do some stuff in the art room."

Charlie nodded. "Later, Picasso."

"Later," I said to his back. As Charlie was swallowed up by the lunchtime crowd, I wondered if I should just follow him. Have lunch with the guys in the band, talk about music, what we should play for the talent show, fight about whether U2 is one of the greatest bands in the history of music or entirely overrated. It was something I would have done a few months ago, just hung out with people who weren't exactly friends but were close enough.

Before Amanda came along, close enough had been fine.

So why wasn't it now?

"**G**od, I *hate* this song." I pressed my hands to my ears to prove my commitment to silencing every note of "Silly Love Songs," which was blasting over the speakers at Aqua.

Amanda took a sip of her espresso. "It is a pretty bad song." She was wearing a ladder of black rubber bracelets on her arm and a short, blond, asymmetrical wig. Whenever my mom has to do some household chore she hates, like vacuuming or cleaning out the fridge, she always blasts old-school Madonna CDs, so I got the reference.

I loved talking about the Beatles with Amanda, and now I leaned across the table with enthusiasm. "You know why it's a bad song? Because Paul McCartney is a crap songwriter."

To indicate her disagreement, Amanda raised her right eyebrow. "'Revolution,' 'Dear Prudence,' 'Rocky Raccoon.' Shall I continue?" Given her agreement that the song sucked, I was surprised by her defense of Paul McCartney.

I waved away her list. "John Lennon wrote every one of those."

"Lennon/McCartney," she corrected. "Read the album cover."

"John Lennon's being man enough to share the credit for those songs with Paul McCartney doesn't make Paul McCartney a decent songwriter. Exhibit A: Wings."

"When they were young, they'd go to parties and just stand in the corner writing songs together." Amanda smiled at the image in her head.

I snorted. "You know what I'd like to see? I'd like to see a transcript of those conversations. 'Hey, Paul, could you try not to write the cheesiest lyrics ever?' 'Sorry, mate, don't think I can do that.'"

"'Each friend represents a world in us, a world possibly not born until they arrive.'" She swirled her spoon around the sides of her cup.

I remained thoroughly unconvinced. "I hate Paul McCartney." When she reraised her eyebrow at what I'd said, I backed off. Slightly. "Okay, I hate the post-Beatles Paul McCartney. Happy?"

Her smile was sad and she shook her head. "You can't hate Paul. Hating Paul is the same as hating John."

What she'd just said was so outrageous I nearly choked on my hot chocolate. "Hating John?! Are you seriously accusing me of hating John?!"

"Friendships like theirs . . ." Amanda linked her ring-laden fingers together to illustrate her point. "They were each changed forever by the other."

"It's too bad Paul wasn't changed a little more. Maybe then his post-Beatles music wouldn't be such garbage."

Still looking at her hands, Amanda spoke slowly. "Maybe it wasn't like that. Maybe John sucked all the genius out of Paul. Maybe Paul grieved so deeply for the end of the Beatles that he never recovered. Or maybe John kept Paul honest and Yoko kept John honest." She shot me a look, knowing I could never resist an opportunity to trash Yoko Ono. "The point is, there'd be no John without Paul. Friends—real friends—they create you as profoundly as your parents."

I felt some of the fight going out of me. "So what you're saying is I don't get to hate Paul anymore?"

"John said it, not me," Amanda pointed out. "Now, let me hear *you* say it."

And for the first time in our friendship, I was the one who quoted something to her. "'Love is the answer.'"

As she raised her cup, I raised mine and we toasted the late, great Lennon by singing the end of the musical line together. "'And you know that for sure.'"

Was that the problem? Had I been changed forever by these friendships? Was I never going to be able to go back to being the Hal I'd been before I knew these people?

Riding home from school on Friday, the watch Amanda had given me in one pocket and my silent cell phone in the other, I felt more sympathy for Paul McCartney than I'd ever dreamed possible. So he'd become a cheesy pop singer after the death of his best friend, so what? At least he didn't spend the rest of his life lying around doing nothing or coming up with bizarre conspiracy theories about John's death.

If only I could say the same thing about myself.

Saturday morning, my dad and I went for a long run, just the two of us. He asked me all about school and the band and what I was painting. All week, I'd kind of been lying in wait, hoping for a chance with him alone. Now I figured I'd let him get all questioned out and then demand to know what he'd meant by his "be careful" from the other night, but when we made the turn onto Briar Lane, my mom and Cornelia were waiting for us at the car.

"You guys are so slow! We've been waiting here forever." Cornelia was standing with her back against the car.

My mom's window was down and she was waving to us. "Who wants to go out for some really un-nutritious pancakes instead of finishing his healthy run?"

"I'd say we've earned us some pancakes," answered my dad, almost gratefully, then Mom added, "Followed by lattes at Just Desserts."

"Awesome," said Dad.

"Awesome *Anna*," winked my mom.

I rolled my eyes. Before you could say, *Tell me what you know, Dad*, we were sitting in the back of the car and headed to Rosie's Diner. Much as I wanted to talk to him, amazing Just Desserts lattes (served by Anna, who really is the world's coolest waitress even if my mom thinks so, too) was at least some consolation for the interruption.

I wasn't alone with him for the rest of the day, and at five he left for a business trip to Toronto. Lying on my bed after we'd hugged good-bye, I kept replaying our conversation. *If I could protect you from every bad thing in the world, I would.* I groaned and rolled onto my back. Naturally my dad didn't know anything. A girl was missing. The vice principal of my school had recently been attacked in his office. Of *course* my dad would tell me to be careful. My thinking his telling me to be careful had something to do with some kind of inside information about Amanda was just one more indication that I was slowly, quietly losing my mind.

"Hal?" My mom pushed open the door to my room as she knocked, which I'd finally accepted was as close as she was ever going to come to knocking *before* entering. Seeing me lying on my bed in my running clothes, she crossed her arms in front of her chest.

"What? I went with Dad. You *saw* me." My mom's refusing to let me go for a run by myself was probably not helping my state of mind.

She didn't relax her stance. "Nobody put you under house arrest, mister. I just don't think it's polite to go to the show dressed like that."

"What show?"

"What do you mean 'what show'?" She stepped into the room and I could see she was dressed in a pair of nice pants and a long sweater, a bright necklace of plastic beads around her neck. "The show you've been working so hard on. I *told* you we were all going to see it Saturday night."

Had my mom told me we were going to *As You Like It* tonight? It wasn't like I'd exactly been focused on every word she spoke at dinner the past few nights, what with trying to figure out everything from how I was going to get Callie and Nia to forgive me to whether or not they, my sister, my parents, and basically everyone I loved was in mortal danger. So, yes, it was possible I could have missed a simple declarative sentence such as, *We are going out as a family Saturday night.*

My mom was still looking at me, eyebrows raised. "Are you at least going to put on a shirt?"

It wasn't like I had anything else to do.

"Something nice," she said as she walked out of my room. "You know it—"

"Shows respect for the performers," we finished together. I'd only been hearing her utter that sentence every time my family went to a concert, play, or dance performance all my conscious life.

"Well, it does," she said, and she pulled my door shut behind her.

Even before we went inside, I could see that the Endeavor lobby was packed with families waiting to go into the auditorium, but of course when we stepped through the front doors, the very first person we saw was Callie's dad. He looked better than he'd looked the last time when I saw him picking up Callie in his truck. He and my mom started chatting and a few minutes later the Riveras were standing next to us. As usual, they were elegantly dressed and managed to give off more of a movie-star vibe than an Endeavor-parent one. Mrs. Rivera started asking my mom if she might be interested in volunteering for some book sale and I almost laughed—was there any cause my mom *wasn't* interested in volunteering for?

I knew the girls were busy with costumes backstage, but I found myself half looking around for them and feeling lonelier than I'd ever remembered feeling.

Cisco Rivera came over with his date and shook my hand. He asked how my painting was going and if there'd been any opportunities that came my way because of the national art contest I'd won. No wonder Cisco was so popular—how did a guy as cool and busy as he was remember that some random freshman who'd been over at his house once had won an art contest months ago?! I was so amazed he remembered my winning that when he introduced me to his date, I didn't register her name. A second later someone called out, "Hey, Cisco," and within seconds, he'd disappeared into a small crowd of people.

It was like watching the mayor of Endeavor chatting with his constituents.

Cisco's date had long dark hair, and as Cisco high-fived a couple of his friends from the soccer team, she gave me a little what-can-you-do-with-a-popular-guy-like-that shrug. I smiled back at her, wondering if I should ask her what her name was again or just hope I could dodge the fact that I hadn't heard it the first time, and as we looked at each other, I suddenly got the weirdest flash that I knew her from somewhere.

Was she an actress? Had I seen her in something like a sitcom or movie?

"You go to Endeavor?" she asked.

I nodded. "How do you know Cisco?" Maybe her answer would help explain this feeling.

"We met in D.C.," she explained. "I go to college there, and Cisco was on a school soccer thing." I realized it was crazy for me to think I knew her. Probably she just reminded me of one of the models in the J.Crew catalogs that seemed to arrive at our house hourly.

The lights dimmed, then came back up, and two girls dressed as courtiers came through the lobby ringing small gold bells.

"Come find your seats. Seats please." The girls made their way through the crowd, which quickly began to thin now that the auditorium doors were open. Normally I would have been annoyed by how my mom put her arm around my shoulders and guided me toward the theater like I was the same age as Cornelia, but tonight I was just lonely enough not to mind her steering me to a seat.

She squeezed my hand as we sat down. "Oh, Hal, it's beautiful." The scrim, lit from behind, seemed to be an opaque wall of dense foliage. I'd wanted to give the audience the impression that they were staring down a corridor of trees in a forest, and I guess I'd succeeded. The truth was, I couldn't really judge if it was any good or not and I didn't really care. The better the show, the better Heidi Bragg was going to look. If there were a way I could have erased every leaf I'd drawn over the past week, returning the Forest of Arden to its prehistoric pre-Hal look, I'd have done so with pleasure.

The house lights dimmed, the scrim rose, and when the stage lights came up, we were in the interior of a nobleman's house.

"As I remember, Adam, it was upon this fashion / bequeathed me by will but poor a thousand crowns, / and, as thou sayest, charged my brother, on his blessing, to breed me well: and there begins my sadness." The guy playing Orlando was actually named Adam, which had been its own inside joke for the cast every time he'd made this speech. Tonight, though, the guy playing Adam and the one playing Oliver managed to get through the scene without cracking themselves up.

Except for the parts where I'd had to listen to Heidi, I'd actually gotten kind of into the play with its crazy plot and its star-crossed lovers and girls dressed as boys and noblemen dressed as shepherds. But the actors might as well have been speaking Japanese—their words barely managed to penetrate my current mood. All I could think about was Callie and Nia working backstage because I'd come up with this brilliant plan to give us the chance to study Amanda's box. Amanda's box that I'd promptly lost. I imagined them thinking of and hating me a little more with each costume change they had to orchestrate. The thought made me literally squirm in my seat, and halfway through the first act, my mom put her hand on my arm and leaned toward me. "Are you okay, honey?" Her voice was a whisper, but the message was loud and clear: *Sit still, Hal.*

"Sorry," I mumbled. As we'd left the house, I'd shoved Amanda's watch in the front pocket of my jeans. Now it dug into my leg, but I knew if I shifted positions one more time my mom would have my head, so I just sat there, glad the pain in my thigh gave me something to focus on besides the pain in my chest.

"I might not sit with you for the second half."

It was the end of intermission, and my mom and Cornelia were headed back into the auditorium. I'd spent the past fifteen minutes looking around the lobby for Callie and Nia before realizing that, of course, they were probably backstage.

Not that it would have mattered if they were standing next to me in the lobby. When people are ignoring you, distance isn't what's keeping you apart.

My mom reached forward and brushed the hair out of my eyes. "You want to sit with your friends, hon?"

"Yeah." As I spoke the word, I realized it wasn't even a lie. I did want to sit with my friends. The problem was, they didn't want to sit with me.

Because they were no longer my friends.

Like she knew there was more to my answer than I was saying, my mom leaned forward and gave me a brief hug. "See you after the show," she said, before she and Cornelia were swallowed up by the crowd.

I thought about leaving the building, but that would have meant either coming back before the play's end or explaining to my paranoid mother why I'd headed out into the night to hoof it home alone rather than just waiting for her to give me a ride. Instead, I headed down the B corridor toward the one place I couldn't imagine feeling lonely no matter how alone I was: the art room.

Normally I'm not one to get the jitters, but as I walked farther and farther from the brightly lit lobby, I found myself wishing the studio were a little closer to the theater. The halls were dark, and though it was a clear night, the moonlight only worked its way so far into the building. By the time I pushed open the unlocked door to the studio, I was feeling more than a little creeped out. The room was lit with a red glow from the bulb that indicates the dark room is in use. Even though I knew nobody could be in there, I didn't bother to hit the light switch—just headed over to the ancient, paint-splattered sofa and threw myself down on it.

Lying on the sofa, I felt the watch jamming into my leg again, and this time I dug into my pocket and pulled it out. In the red light, the metal took on a lurid glow, and I traced my finger over the inscription I'd looked at so many times before. *"I know you (x2) know me."*

I felt like throwing the watch across the room. Dipping it into paint thinner. Crushing it with the paper cutter.

Smashing and torturing and squeezing it until it was forced to relinquish its meaning.

The Saint Catherine's carnival to raise funds for needy children, taking place on the town green, was definitely an event I could stand to miss, but there was no convincing Amanda of that.

"It'll be fun, Hal. Don't you want to have fun?" She was standing at my front door wearing a pair of black leather pants, a black leather motorcycle jacket, and black motorcycle boots. It was very don't-mess-with-me attire, and hers was a very don't-mess-with-me voice.

"Carnivals aren't fun," I corrected her. "They're depressing."

"No, actually, sitting inside on a beautiful fall day is depressing. Carnivals are fun."

In the end, it was easier to get on my bike and follow her to the green than to try and convince her I didn't want to spend my afternoon eating cotton candy and trying to win tacky stuffed animals by hitting things with hammers or throwing quarters at chickens or whatever it is you do to win stuff at carnivals.

To my surprise, the carnival wasn't nearly as awful as I'd imagined. There were a million little kids there laughing and running around and getting their faces painted and generally having a total blast, and the people running the games and rides were regular people, not the circus freaks I'd been picturing in my mind. By the time we got to the game where you shoot water at a duck to win a huge, stuffed bear, I was actually kind of into it.

I watched as Amanda wrapped her hands around the handle of the water gun and slipped her index finger against the trigger. She squinted at the smiling plastic ducks as they floated past us on their plastic river, and the intensity of her stare made me glad I wasn't one of them. Out of nowhere, without turning to look at me, she announced, "I want to talk to you about your art."

And suddenly I felt like I had a whole lot more in common with those ducks than I'd thought. "Let's not and say we did," I suggested, trying to keep my voice light. I reached into the bag I was holding and offered some caramel-covered popcorn in her direction. "Cracker Jack, anyone?"

"We're not talking snack options, Hal, we're talking about your art." She squeezed the trigger and a duck flipped onto its back as a bell rang, signaling her success.

"No, *you're* talking about my art. I'm just trying to enjoy this beautiful fall day." I breathed deeply and made a show of looking around me. "Smell that crisp air?"

Amanda ignored my meteorologistic commentary. "It's time for you to put yourself out there, Bennett." Bam! Another duck bit the dust.

Watching Amanda kill helpless plastic waterfowl while she put the screws to me about my art was more than I could take. I turned and leaned my back against the counter, staring off into some vague near distance. "Yeah, about that. I'm thinking I'd like to be discovered *posthumously*. Like—hey, look at this! We thought he was just, you know, an amazing auto mechanic, but it turns out he was the artistic genius of the twenty-first century."

Bam! The click of the plastic flipping over and the ding of the bell ringing let me know what had happened even if I couldn't see it.

"Hal, what you know about cars would fit on a three-by-five index card. And as far as posthumous discovery, you know what you get to be when you're dead?"

"Famous?" I offered.

"Dead," she corrected me. To emphasize her point (as if it needed emphasis), she shot and killed another innocent plastic duck.

"Isn't there some kind of limit on this game?" I asked, gesturing at the booth we stood in front of. "Haven't you maxed out or something?"

"Don't change the subject, Hal." There was more than a whisper of annoyance in her voice. "It's time for you to let people see your work."

"I *am* changing the subject, Amanda." She wasn't the only one with the right to get pissed off. "And I'll show people my work when I'm good and ready."

Still holding the gun, she turned to glare at me. "Which will be when, never?"

"Not that it's any of your business, but yeah, maybe. If I want to die with a studio full of canvases and a storage space full of sketchbooks that nobody has ever seen, that's my right."

"No, Hal, it isn't!" Was it my imagination or was she jonesing to spin the water gun in my direction and blast me as thoroughly as she had the ducks? "When you have talent, you have to put yourself out in the world. 'To whom much is given, much is expected.'"

Now we were both glaring at each other. "And who, exactly, are you to decide to whom much has been given?"

"Oh, don't give me the whole, 'Little old me, what could I possibly have to offer anyone' routine."

"It's not a routine!" I was so mad I chucked my Cracker Jack to the ground. "My art is private! I'll put it out in the world when I'm ready to put it out in the world, and if that's never, so be it."

Amanda stepped around the gun and thrust her finger into my chest. Hard. "Too late, Hal. I already showed your sketches to Mr. Harper. He's entering you in the National Art Society's high school competition."

"What the—" I stared at her, too shocked to finish my sentence.

Amanda took her finger away from my chest. "It's time to be a part of the world, Hal. Time to step up. 'You're either on the bus or you're off it.'" She walked backward a few paces, then lifted her hands up as if asking a question.

"But—"

"And I'm not just talking about your art," she finished.

Before I could say a thing (and what would I have said? Thank

166

you? To hell with you?) she'd turned around and headed to where we'd left our bikes.

By the time I got my head clear enough to follow her, she was long gone.

"I still have no idea what you meant!" I shouted to the empty art room.

And to my amazement, out of the darkness, a voice answered. "Of course you don't. I haven't said anything yet."

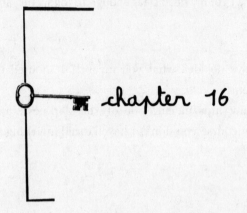

chapter 16

I shot off the couch and spun around faster than if Mr. Richards had been standing over me with a stopwatch.

Amanda!

But the person who was standing in the open doorway wasn't Amanda. It was Callie.

My heart was pounding, and I could barely swallow my mouth was so dry. Despite how psyched I was to see her, fear made my voice sharp. "You scared the crap out of me."

"Who were you talking to?"

"I . . ." How could I answer that? *The past. I was talking to the past.* "No one."

"Oh."

I half sat, half fell down on the couch, still breathing hard from my shock at hearing an answer to the question I'd been asking of a person inside my head. A second later Callie came over and sat beside me.

She took a deep breath, then spoke quickly, almost as if she'd planned what she wanted to say. I steeled myself for the attack I feared was coming.

"So I owe you an enormous apology and I'm really sorry I was so mean and I hope you can forgive me."

"I . . . wait a second, what?" About to launch into a major apology myself, I was so totally unprepared for what she said that it took a minute before the meaning of her words sank in.

This time she turned to me, her skin pale in the red light of the bulb. "I said I'm sorry."

"You're sorry," I repeated. There was a brief silence. "Okay, I'm confused. What do you have to be sorry *for* exactly?"

Callie bit her lip for a second. As though she hadn't rehearsed *this* part of what she wanted to say, her words came slowly now. "I am so totally the last person in the world to judge someone who falls under the spell of Heidi Bragg."

"You . . ." I couldn't decide which was more incredible— that Callie sounded as if she might be considering forgiving me or that she'd described so perfectly Heidi's power. The spell of Heidi Bragg. That was exactly what it felt like—as if I'd fallen under a spell.

Which didn't make what I'd done any less heinous.

"Callie, I am so, so sorry. I—"

"Shh." She touched her finger to her lips. "Stop, okay? It could have happened to anyone. Heidi's smart. Scary smart. She finds people's weak spots and she exploits them."

I saw Heidi's sorrowful expression, heard her fake remorse

about the way she'd treated Callie. She hadn't tried to flirt with me or flatter me. She'd known doing either of those things would have had zero effect. Somehow she'd realized there was only one way to get me to listen her—to distract me—and it was to pretend to regret what she'd done to Callie.

She'd found my weak spot and she'd exploited it.

"Thanks." It was all I could think of to say, but I had the feeling it was enough.

Callie had shut the door to the art room behind her, and now it flew open, slamming against the wall. "We have exactly eight and a half minutes."

Nia.

"I'll take that as hello," I said. Callie's forgiveness gave me the confidence to smile at Nia.

"You'll take it all right," said Nia, but she was sort of smiling, too. "So this *is* where you came to wallow. Callie was right."

"Hey, I resent that. I was not *wallowing*."

"Whatever." Nia waved away my protest. "The point is, we now have"—she glanced at her phone—"less than eight and a half minutes to figure out how we're going to get that box back from Heidi Bragg and her I-Goonies. I's for *idiot*, right?" Nia addressed her question to Callie.

"I think it's for *I will be underestimated at your own risk*," Callie corrected.

"I think you're right," Nia said, and from her voice, I could tell that even she was daunted by the impossibility of our getting Amanda's box back from Heidi.

"Hal, will you *stop doing that*?! It's driving me *crazy*." Nia spoke in a growl.

"Stop doing *what*?" I'd just been sitting there thinking about how we were never going to see Amanda's box again, but unless Nia had suddenly developed ESP, the odds were she wasn't railing against my negative thoughts.

"*That.*" She mimed flicking something with her finger, and I realized I must have been opening and shutting the watch without realizing it. "You do it all the time."

"I do? Sorry," I said, and I started to shove the watch back into my pocket.

"Yeah, I've been meaning to ask—what is that?" asked Callie, reaching for the watch.

"It's a pocket watch," said Nia.

As Nia came over to where Callie and I were sitting, I suddenly remembered Frieda's warning. This was bad. This was very bad.

Taking it from me, Callie held the watch up to her face and squinted at the inscription in the dim light. "I know you," she read.

"Guys," I announced, "we need to separate."

Callie was too focused on what she was reading to pay attention to what I'd just said, but Nia heard me.

"What are you talking about? We just got back *together*, you idiot."

"No," I insisted. "I mean, yes. But we shouldn't have. It's dangerous for us to be together."

I was about to explain everything that Frieda had told me

when Callie said, "'I know you. You know me.' I don't get it."

My head snapped around to look at her. "What did you just say?"

"I don't get it," Callie repeated.

"Before that."

"Um, 'I know you. You know me.'"

"That's not what it says," I told her. "It says, 'I know you,' then 'x2' in parentheses, then 'know me.'"

Callie shook her head and showed me the all-too-familiar inscription. "The 'x2' in parentheses means multiply the item immediately proceeding it by two, in this case, the 'you.' It's algebraic notation."

"Oh my god," I said.

Because suddenly I knew where the inscription came from.

Callie laughed, misunderstanding my amazement. "It's not that big a deal. You just—"

"No, you don't understand! I know what it means now. 'I know you. You know me.'"

The girls stared at me blankly.

"This watch." I pointed at it. "It's from Amanda. And the inscription—it's a song." I threw my head back, unsure about whether I wanted to laugh or cry. "It's a Beatles song. 'I know you. You know me.' Those are the lyrics."

"Amanda," Callie whispered.

"Um, okay," said Nia. "Not exactly the most exciting but, you know, who am I to criticize the Beatles? I mean, 'Michelle' might be fairly mundane, but 'Day in the Life—'"

"The message." I held out my hand in the universal signal

for stop. I needed time, literally, for all the gears in my own head to spin. "The message is *come together*. She's telling us to work together to find her." The song played in my head and I almost shouted the chorus at Nia and Callie. "'Come together, right now, over me!' It's not *dangerous* for us to work together. It's *crucial*!"

"What are you talking about?" Nia asked.

"Why would it be dangerous?" Callie added.

"Frieda said—" But they didn't know about my trip to see Frieda. They didn't know because I hadn't told them. And I hadn't told them because I'd been so eager to be the one to find Amanda that I'd missed the most important tool for finding her.

Us. The three of us. Together.

A small buzz began, growing louder over the next few seconds.

"We have less than a minute to get backstage," Nia observed, pushing a button on her phone and standing up.

Callie jumped up. "Wait! We didn't figure out how to get the box back."

"Oh, but we did," Nia said, moving toward the door.

"We did?" I asked.

"Together," Nia prompted, and Callie and I looked at each other and then back at her, neither of us getting it.

Nia shook her head, clearly amazed by how dense we were. "Where are we all going to be *together* in less than an hour?"

"Um, nowhere?" Callie offered.

"Um, cast party?" Nia corrected her. "But I like the sarcasm. I must be rubbing off on you." She gestured with her hand for Callie to join her at the door, and Callie did.

Suddenly I remembered. "The cast party's at Heidi's."

"Oh, no! No way!" Callie wagged her index finger at Nia. "I don't mean to be a drama queen or anything, but I promised myself I'd never set foot in that house again."

Close enough that she could reach out and grab Callie's hand, Nia did just that, pulling Callie through the door. "Yes, objection duly noted, okay?"

As she and Callie disappeared into the corridor, Nia called to me over her shoulder. "Get your mom to drop you at Heidi's after the play."

The door closed behind them, leaving me alone in the art room, so amazed at everything that had just happened I fell against the back of the sofa. Here I was, right where I'd been when Callie surprised me, yet I felt so completely different I might as well have traveled halfway around the world. I touched my forearm where the tattoo of a cougar was fading a little every day.

One man in his time plays many parts.
You're on the bus or you're off the bus.
The time for me to be the loner had come to an end.
Now it was time for me to be a friend.

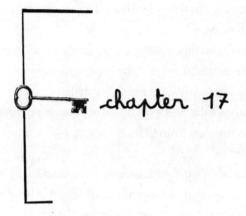

chapter 17

"You do realize it could be anywhere, don't you?"

We were standing on the Braggs' front lawn. As it turned out, Mom had given me and Callie a ride, and Nia had hopped out of her parents' car less than a minute after my family's Subaru pulled away. In spite of my happiness at being reunited with Callie and Nia, standing there, the brightly lit windows of the house's enormous interior casting shadows on the perfectly cropped grass, I couldn't help being more than a little overwhelmed by our task.

"The only question is how we're going to get past Heidi in the first place. Once that's accomplished, we're golden." Nia's voice was so confident I couldn't believe we had the same agenda. It was like I was planning on breaking into Fort Knox and she was hoping to get herself a Limonata, which I happened to remember was her favorite drink. No common soda for Nia. "Oh, don't worry about that; Heidi's going to be late," Callie said casually.

I was totally confused by that. "How can she be late? The party's at her house."

"She'll stay in her room getting ready," Callie explained, brushing her hands together. "She'll want to make an entrance."

"But it's her house," I repeated stupidly.

Suddenly Callie and Nia burst out laughing, like I'd just uttered the funniest thing since Abbott and Costello's *Who's on First*.

"Sorry, Hal," Callie said, covering her mouth with her hand but unable to prevent another burst of laughter from escaping.

"Yeah, sorry," Nia echoed, laughing, too.

"Let me guess—I'm being such a guy, right?"

"Something like that," Callie assured me, patting my arm as she and Nia, emboldened rather than daunted by what a dolt they were working with, started up the lawn toward the Braggs' house.

There were a few cars parked in the driveway, meaning either the Braggs had a fleet of automobiles or that some of the older cast members had already arrived. As Callie pushed the front door open without knocking, voices from inside made it clear we were not the first guests to show, which was a relief. The bigger the crowd, the easier it would be to disappear.

Everything as far as the eye could see was white or off-white—the sofas, the rugs, even the walls, which didn't seem to be painted so much as . . . upholstered in a pale beige silky fabric. To my right, a bunch of people were gathered around an enormous glass table in the gigantic dining room. To my left was a sunken living room that was itself roughly the square footage of my entire downstairs. For once I was glad to be no good at math—just thinking about calculating the odds of finding a twelve-inch-by-twelve-inch box in all that space was enough to make me want to turn around and go home. Forget the fact that the box could be anywhere in the house. It could be anywhere *not* in the house.

"Should we split up?" I suggested, trying to silence the voices of doom in my head. "Text if we find something?"

At this suggestion, Nia spun to face us. "Give me your phone numbers."

Callie's face was bewildered. "Nia, what are you talking about—you've called me a million times by now. You *have* my number."

Nia pulled an iPhone from the tiny handbag that swung from her wrist.

"You got an iPhone!" Callie nearly gasped.

In response, Nia wacked Callie on the butt with her bag. "No, you shallow I-Girl, it's my brother's. He loaned it to me."

"That's *former* I-Girl," Callie corrected her. "And where's *your* phone?"

"Out of juice," Nia explained, and she prepared to enter our numbers into Cisco Rivera's phone. Her eyes gleamed in a way that made me wonder if Cisco *knew* he'd loaned his sister his iPhone. "Now, scoot."

* * *

Of course Nia and Callie were right that it made total sense for me to go upstairs and risk running into Heidi and the other I-Girls. Our little scene in the auditorium notwithstanding, I hardly had the history with Heidi and her flunkies that Nia and Callie did. Still, that fact did nothing to make my heart pound less furiously as I pushed open the bedroom door of the Orion police chief.

Oh, sorry, sir, I was just looking for the bathroom. Now, really, I don't think we need those handcuffs, it was an honest mistake. Sir! Sir! Chief Bragg, don't I get even one phone call—

I tried to shake this image from my head, but by the time I was literally on my hands and knees under the desk in what must have been a guest bedroom, it was getting increasingly hard to come up with a plausible story to explain my behavior. *I think I might have left my coat last time I was over. When was that, you say? Oh, uh, I'm pretty sure it was never.*

I'd been looking for at least forty-five minutes, and all I'd learned was that Mrs. Bragg had so many shoes they literally could not be contained within the more than dozen closets upstairs—when I opened the closet door in the guest room, a box dropped onto my head and red shoes exploded, the heels so spiky the impact of one with my head brought tears to my eyes. I was rubbing the spot on my scalp where a small lump was swiftly growing when my phone buzzed.

MEET ME DOWNSTAIRS IN HALLWAY BTWN
KITCHEN & LIVING ROOM.

I'd never been so happy to do anything as I was to flee the upstairs of the Braggs' house. Walking by a closed door I'd passed before, I concluded from the Miley Cyrus now blasting from within that it was Heidi's, and I was relieved to know she was still sequestered in her room, at least for the moment.

Moment, unfortunately, being the key word, I realized, as I took the winding stairs two at a time.

"What are you doing, Hal?"

I spun around so fast I'm pretty sure I heard something in my ankle pop. Just looking for the bathroom. *Just looking for the bathroom. Just . . .*

But the person addressing me from the archway between the foyer and the Braggs' dining room wasn't a member of the Bragg family. It was a sophomore girl who'd played one of the courtiers in exile, Theresa Ax, also known as Terri.

Was she a good friend of Heidi's, good enough that she'd know there was no reason for me to be wandering around upstairs in Heidi's house?

"Um . . ." She was holding a sandwich and looking at me in this really intense way. Maybe it was just the guilt talking, but to me her look definitely said, *I'm onto you. . . .* I decided to punt. "Sorry, what did you say?"

"I *said,* what are you *doing* here?"

Here like upstairs at Heidi's house? Here like in the foyer?

"I . . ." It was one thing to tell Chief Bragg I was looking for the bathroom, another to casually inform Terri the sophomore girl that I'd been standing somewhere with my pants down.

She flipped her long black hair over her shoulder in a way

that made me wonder if she was auditioning for a position in the soon-to-be-formed I-Girl sophomore division. If that were the case, I hoped for her sake that she spelled Terri with an i and not a y. "I don't think I've, like, *ever* seen you at a party before."

"Oh, well . . ." My ankle was throbbing and I felt the buzz of my phone vibrating in my jacket pocket.

She took a bite of her sandwich and looked at me. "We should seriously hang out."

Was this another Heidi Bragg trick? Would I ever again be able to talk to anyone without wondering what her ulterior motive might be? "Yeah, sure," I said. Kitchens were usually near dining rooms, weren't they? That was how it worked in my house, anyway. I looked over Terri's shoulder—sure enough, there was a swinging door behind her.

Kitchen.

"I'll catch you later," I said, then turned and practically flew through the swinging door.

The kitchen was crowded with people from the play. For a second I didn't see any of the I-Girls, but then I looked again and, out of the corner of my eye, spotted the one with the dark hair—I was pretty sure her name was Traci or Kelli. She was pouring some diet soda into a couple of glasses, and as I headed toward the door on the opposite side of the room, the one I was sincerely hoping would lead me to the hallway Callie was talking about, I thought she might have looked up and seen me. Right as we made eye contact, Nia, coming from the side, bumped into her. Traci/Kelli stumbled and several glasses of soda spilled down the front of her shirt.

Traci/Kelli's squeal of fury was like something you'd hear in a documentary about wildlife of the Amazon basin. I took a step toward them, ready to help out if she needed me, but Nia began to laugh.

Traci/Kelli's eyes widened with amazement. "You're *laughing*, you freak?"

Nia crossed her arms over her chest, still laughing. "Yes, I-Girl, I am."

A couple of people standing around laughed briefly at Nia's retort as Traci/Kelli rattled the ice in one of the near-empty glasses in her direction. "You'll regret this!"

Nia shook her head mock-regretfully. "You know something? I really don't think I will."

As I pushed through a door and out of the kitchen, I could not help but smile. I found myself standing at one end of a short hallway, empty except for Callie, who was standing about halfway down it staring at the wall.

"Hey," she said, glancing over and seeing it was me before going back to looking at the wall in front of her.

"Hey," I said. "Nia's kicking ass and taking names." I went to stand beside her and see what she was staring at.

The sight nearly made me gag.

The wall was covered, almost literally, with photos of the Bragg family, particularly Brittney Bragg. There must have been five hundred pictures of them—the Braggs on a ski slope, goggles around their necks, parkas unzipped despite the cold that turned their breath white. Brittney Bragg in the shortest shorts I'd ever seen cracking a bottle over the bow of . . . I leaned forward and squinted. *Bragging Rights*. Of course. There was a series of faux-casual black-and-white pictures of the family, Brittney in a crisp, white, collared shirt, Chief Bragg in jeans and a dark T-shirt. Heidi wore a sundress, and her little brother was in what looked to be a soccer uniform.

Then there was the overseas portion of the wall: Chief and Mrs. Bragg at the Great Wall of China, the Acropolis, in front of the towering cruise ship that had no doubt delivered them to such exotic locales. In every photo, the two or three or four Braggs were smiling broadly, looking, for all the world, like the all-American family they were pretending to be.

I shook my head in amazement. "How is it possible for pure evil to look so happy-go-lucky?"

"This shouldn't be here," Callie stated firmly.

"I mean, why limit ourselves to the pictures? The whole *development* is a scourge on the face of the planet."

She shook her head. "But I mean, specifically, this wall."

"I hear what you're saying, but, well, you know, without walls houses kind of . . . fall down." Quickly, I added, "I'm kidding."

"Maybe with all that knowledge you should consider a career in architecture." A small smile played at the corner of Callie's mouth.

She stepped forward and knocked at the wall, then shook her head. "I don't even know what I'm knocking for. But they always do it in the movies."

"Do you think it's hollow?" I stepped forward and knocked

also, but the wall sounded like a wall.

"No, it's not that. Look." She pulled me back in the direction I'd come from and opened a door I hadn't even noticed when I'd walked past. Inside was a laundry room.

Not quite sure what Callie was showing me, I looked around. But the room we were in just seemed like your basic, run-of-the-mill laundry room—washer, dryer, rack for hanging stuff. There were boxes of detergent and fabric softener on a shelf above the machines and an iron on an ironing board that stuck out of the wall next to a small door that looked like it might have led to a closet.

"Got it?" asked Callie.

"Um, okay, yeah."

"Now, look at this." She pulled me back into the hallway; a few feet past where we'd been standing, she opened another door. The room reminded me of the family room at Nia's—except that here the TV was approximately the size of the screen at your local multiplex. There was a stereo and a wall of built-in bookcases that, instead of books, held even more photos, mostly of Brittney Bragg smiling with local celebrities and politicians.

Callie watched me watching the room. "What do you notice?" she asked finally.

"That the Braggs are even more culturally illiterate and less aware of their relative insignificance in the world than I'd ever imagined?"

"True," Callie agreed. "But what else?"

I had the feeling she wasn't asking about the décor, which

was a little too much chrome and glass for my taste, so I just said, "I give up."

"Don't feel bad," she assured me. "I've been here a million times and I never noticed it, either." She thought for a second. "Here's a hint: How big would you say this room is?"

I looked from one wall to the other, then calculated in my head. "I'm not great at this—maybe twenty feet long and fifteen feet wide."

"Yeah, that's about what I figured. Now, come back into the hallway." I followed her and we stood where we'd been when I first found her. "What do you notice this time?"

I looked at the wall. I looked at the door to the laundry room. I looked back to the door of the den. And, finally, I saw what Callie had seen.

"There's extra space!"

Callie was nodding excitedly. Again I looked at the wall and calculated the size of the two rooms we'd just been in. Even though I'm no expert at judging space, there were at least ten feet unaccounted for. Which meant—

Callie put her hand on my arm and we turned to look at each other.

"A hidden room!" I whispered.

Callie's eyes sparkled with triumph. "And what do you want to bet our box is in it?"

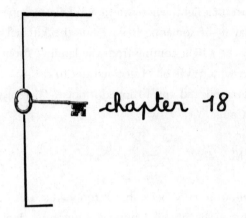

chapter 18

Callie and I split up; she headed back to the den and I went into the laundry room. Now that Callie had pointed it out to me, the unaccounted-for space was completely obvious—unless the walls of the Braggs' house were more than eight feet thick, there was something between me and Callie, and it wasn't just a bookcase.

I started making my way along the wall, remembering from days spent reading my dad's old Hardy Boy novels that the important thing was to check every square inch. Except for a couple of framed movie posters and a wooden molding at about waist height, there didn't seem to be any place to hide a doorknob. I opened the small closet, empty except for yet another framed photo of Mrs. Bragg on the wall. This one was of her in a pair of running shorts and a jogging bra with what looked like a medal hanging on a ribbon around her neck.

My god, did these people never get enough of themselves?

I felt along the walls of the closet wondering if it was too risky to turn on a light. There was a window that opened onto the back lawn—if someone looked out the kitchen window, would they see a light coming from the laundry room window and wonder why it was on? I decided not to risk it.

My phone buzzed and I flipped it open. There was a message from Callie.

NOTHING. U?

I was about to type back that I, too, had struck out, when by the light of the phone I noticed something. Holding the illuminated screen open to the wall, I was able to see, nearly hidden in the seam of the wood trim and plaster wall, the tiniest lock I'd ever seen. Hands shaking, I texted Callie back.

SOMETHING.

An instant later, she was next to me in the closet and we were both staring at the lock.

"Okay, okay," she whispered. "That's the lock."

"Now we just need the key."

"That's a big just," she pointed out.

"Think," I said. "If you were Chief Bragg, where would you hide a key?"

"Um, the police station? My key ring?"

"You're assuming it's a key only he needs. What if it's one

he *and* Mrs. Bragg use? Or what if it's one the whole family uses for this secret room?"

Callie thought for a second. "It would have to be someplace central. Someplace everyone could get it."

I nodded, then added, "And it's small, right? So you'd want to keep it near the lock."

"Because if you dropped it, it would be hard to find."

"Exactly. You wouldn't want to have to carry it all over the place."

We turned in sync and looked back at the laundry room. When I'd first seen it, the space had seemed pristine and relatively empty—neatly folded piles of towels, jugs of cleansers with their handles turned out. Now that I was considering searching it for a key the size of a Band-Aid, it suddenly seemed enormous and cluttered.

"Okay," I announced, hoping I sounded more confident than I felt. "Let's do it."

But fifteen minutes later, we'd had zero luck. Feeling totally defeated, Callie and I sat with our backs against the washing machine. We stared, demoralized, at the wall with the lock, the Braggs' secret room so close and yet so far. The smiling, medal-clad Mrs. Bragg hanging in the closet seemed to be mocking our attempts to best her and her family.

Out of nowhere, Callie said, "Mrs. Bragg has a seriously sick body."

I glanced up at the photo. Objectively, I suppose Callie was right, but Brittney Bragg, like her daughter, had always left me cold.

"I guess," I said.

"And she's so discreet," Callie added, indicating on her own body how little of Mrs. Bragg the jogging bra covered. "Oh, am I showing off my *body*?" She giggled an imitation of Brittney Bragg. "I had no *idea*."

And suddenly I jumped to my feet. "Oh my god, I can't believe we missed it."

"What?" Callie scrambled to her feet, watching as I crossed the small room, stood in the closet, and took the photo from its hook.

"I'm sure you can get a signed one from the studio," Callie said, her voice dripping sarcasm. "'Dear Hal—Love ya, baby! Brittney.'"

"No, no, don't you see?" I felt along the back of the picture, sliding my hand under the clips that held it in its frame.

"See what?"

A second later, my fingers felt what they'd been seeking. In the bit of light that came in through the crack under the door, Callie saw the key I was holding up for her to examine.

"But . . . how did you . . . ?" Callie's eyes were wide with amazement.

I hung the photo back on the wall and slipped the key into the lock. As I'd known it would, it slid in easily. Hearing the sound of a bolt sliding back, I turned to Callie, an enormous smile splitting my face. "In what universe would Brittney Bragg put a picture of herself looking super fly in the back of a closet?"

And with that rhetorical question, I pushed open the door to the Bragg family's secret room.

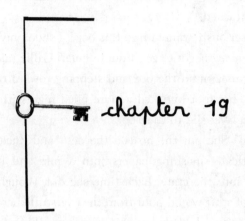

chapter 19

As we'd expected, the room was small, roughly the same dimensions as the laundry room. But that was where the similarities ended. If the laundry room and the rest of the Bragg house were pristine, almost sterile, this room was piled high with clutter—boxes overflowed their tops, files were stacked on the desk in the room's center, and the shelves that lined the walls were bowed under the weight of all the papers they held.

"Look!" Callie was pointing across the room to a small wooden chair.

On it was Amanda's box.

As soon as we were standing next to the box, we could see that someone had been working very, very hard to open it. On the chair next to it were a screwdriver and a hammer, and whether those had been the tools used or they were next up at bat I couldn't tell, but something sharp and strong had definitely been jammed into the pristine wood. I felt nauseated looking at the gouged edges, like it was Amanda herself who had been attacked.

"They seriously wanted into this box." I shook my head.

"We've *seriously* got to get it out of here," Callie said, wrapping her arms around the box and stepping toward the door. As she did, her foot knocked a crate piled high with papers, and the top layer slid to the floor.

"Damn!" She put the box on the desk and knelt on the floor, frantically mashing papers into a pile and dumping them back into the crate. Each time she did, though, a new avalanche of stuff would pour from the overstuffed crate.

"Wait. Wait." I knelt beside Callie, smoothing out some of the papers that had gotten wrinkled while Callie pushed against the stuff inside the crate to make space for them.

As frantically as I was working to flatten out the sheets of paper, I tried to glance at them, too. The first one meant nothing to me. It was a map of a city I'd never heard of—Saint Cloud or Saint Calude, I was reading too fast to be sure—with a small yellow X on a street, the name of which I didn't catch. Next was a receipt from what seemed to be a gas station, followed by a cell phone bill.

"Callie, I'm going to text Nia. I think we should pass her the box from the laundry room window or else someone might—"

"What the hell?!"

I looked up. Callie was sitting back on her heels, holding what looked like a photograph. Crawling over to her side,

I looked at the picture of two young girls, each standing astride a bicycle. In the background, I could just make out the Washington Monument.

I studied the picture for a minute. "Hey, is that—"

Callie's hand was shaking so hard it was difficult to see the girls' faces, but I was pretty sure one of the girls was Heidi Bragg. I took the photo from Callie and held it close.

"It's Brittney." Callie's voice was oddly flat, like she was half asleep. I turned to look at her, and the blankness of her voice was matched by the blankness in her eyes.

"Callie? Are you okay?"

Finger shaking, Callie pointed at the photo in my hand. "That's Brittney Bragg." I looked where she was pointing and I saw that she was right. The girl looked a little like Heidi, but the jaw was one hundred percent Brittney. Plus, the bike she was on was an old-fashioned one with a banana seat, the kind my mom had as a kid. I couldn't see Heidi, no matter how young she was, riding a bike that was so last century.

"Who's the other girl?" I asked, wishing I could say something that would remove the stricken look from Callie's face.

"That's my mom," she said.

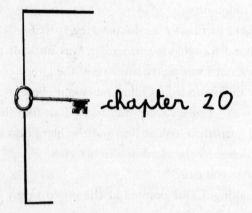

chapter 20

My phone buzzed and I grabbed it from my pocket, asking as I did, "Your mom and Brittney Bragg were friends when they were kids?"

"That's the thing," Callie said. "They weren't. I mean, my mom never said anything about knowing Brittney when they were younger."

For a second I was confused by the unfamiliar number that had sent me a text, but then I remembered that Nia had her brother's phone.

FIND ANYTHING?

I quickly texted back, describing as best I could the location of the laundry room window. Finished, I turned to Callie, still staring at the picture.

"We have to get out of here."

Callie nodded but didn't speak. I went over to the desk and grabbed the box, amazed again by how easily Callie had carried something so heavy. As we made our way to the door, Callie pointed to a small white case about the size of a mini-fridge that neither of us had noticed before. It was plugged into the wall and had a glass front. Inside were—

"Is that . . . *blood*?" Callie knelt down on one knee and I crouched beside her as best I could without putting the box down.

Sure enough, inside the case, which I could see now was a refrigerator, were vials of a thick red substance, each clearly labeled with a number followed by a series of letters. I found myself thinking of Thornhill's files and wishing I could compare the numbers and letters on his files with those on these vials. Was it just a coincidence that everywhere I turned someone seemed to be keeping track of people and things with long letter/number combinations?

With the blood samples was an orange plastic prescription bottle, like the kind my antibiotics came in when I got sinus infections. I squinted at the label, and as I read the name of the prescribing physician, my heart stopped. "Callie?"

She'd started to stand up, but at the sound of her name, she squatted back down and looked where my finger was pointing. "'Dr. Joy,'" she read. Callie turned to me, not bothering to push out of her eyes the hair that had fallen in her face. "This is the most disgusting thing I've ever seen. Let's get out of here."

I nodded and followed her through the door of the office

into the laundry room. As quickly as I could, I put the key back where I'd found it, then replaced the photo on its hook. Brittney Bragg's smile, which had seemed self-satisfied before, suddenly looked terrifying. I had an insane image of her drinking the vials of blood—half TV anchor, half vampire—before Callie shut the door to the closet and hid Mrs. Bragg from view. A second later, I was hoisting up the window and looking at Nia, who was frantically texting into her brother's iPhone.

"Nia, it's okay, we're here," I hissed.

To my surprise, Nia didn't stop typing. "Nia, you can stop texting us. We're right here." I leaned out the window with the box in my arms.

"I'm not texting you," Nia said, not turning to look at me.

"Then who—"

"Send. And Send. And Send. And . . ." Muttering to herself that way, she was like a woman possessed.

"Nia, this is heavy." I raised my voice and she finally looked up, then reached out her hands to take the box, saying, "Oh, sorry," almost as if the box were somehow an afterthought.

I couldn't resist a little pride in my and Callie's success. "Pretty cool, right?" I asked, grinning. Now that I was half out of the house, I could hear the sound of more cars pulling up to the Braggs'. It sounded like every single cast member had decided to come to the party.

Still typing into Cisco's phone, Nia said, "I'm sorry, you want me to admire you for retrieving something that you lost in the first place?"

Okay, clearly I should have resisted. "Fair point." I slid myself back inside the laundry room. "We'll meet you out front in five."

As I put my hands on the screen to drop it down, Nia said, "If you have trouble finding me in the crowd, meet me at the corner."

Had Nia been in a play with a cast twice the size of the one I'd worked on? I couldn't really see how we'd be unable to find her but I just said, "Okay, the corner," and shut the screen.

When I turned around, Callie was still holding the photo of her mom and Brittney. Sensing my eyes on her, she said, "Don't tell me I shouldn't have taken it."

That was pretty much the last thing I would ever have told Callie. If my mom disappeared, I'd take anything I could find that reminded me of her.

"Callie, of course you should have taken it." I put my hand on her shoulder and together we looked at the picture of the smiling girls.

"Can I tell you something?" Her voice was quiet and shaky, and I had the feeling she was trying not to cry. Without waiting for me to answer, Callie continued. "It's been so warm all week, so yesterday, I went up to the attic to get some summer stuff. . . ." Just thinking about Callie doing that made my heart hurt for her—twice a year my mom suddenly announces it's time to put away (or take out) our winter clothes; she spends a whirlwind weekend putting cedar blocks in duffle bags of warm clothes and washing stuff that she decides smells "like the basement," and next thing I know the sweaters in my drawers have magically been transformed into T-shirts or my shorts have become jeans.

If she disappeared from our lives, who would do that?

Callie continued. "When I opened this trunk that has all my T-shirts and stuff, on the inside of the top was a . . ." She gestured to indicate something spread out across a surface. "You know those stars you can stick up on your ceiling to make constellations? The kind that glow in the dark?"

I nodded. Cornelia had some in her room. Since my mom had put them there, and since her idea of astronomy is limited to the sentence, "Aren't the stars pretty tonight?" I wasn't sure they were exactly in the shape of constellations, but I knew what Callie was talking about.

"Well, she'd used them to make a star map. Do you know what a star map is? It's a map that shows where the stars are at a particular place and time."

I nodded and she went on. "Well, the star map in the trunk was the Orion sky. In spring. And . . ." Callie sniffed. "At first I thought, you know, maybe it was like a private joke about when she got out our summer stuff. But with everything that's happened"—she gestured in a way I knew was meant to indicate Amanda, Thornhill, her mother's disappearance, the stolen box—"I got this crazy idea that maybe it's a message. That it means something I'm supposed to understand."

"Oh, Callie." I pushed her hair back from her face. The sound of cars honking at one another filtered through the closed window, and when Callie glanced at me, I could see that her cheek was wet. I wiped at it gently, wishing there was something more I could do.

"She'll come home, Callie. She's safe and she's going to come home."

Suddenly Callie shook herself and wiped at her other cheek with the back of her hand. "I know that," she said, nodding her head vigorously. "I do." She turned to me and gave a sad half smile. "I just miss her, you know?"

Now it was my turn to nod.

"So let's get this show on the road, okay?" Callie's voice was normal again, and I could tell she was as okay as she was claiming to be. From the other side of the laundry room door, the sound of voices could be heard, louder than before.

"Sounds like the party's in full swing," I observed.

Callie stepped in front of me and crossed the room. When I reached her side, she bumped me gently. "Hey! Can you believe we made it in and out of there without getting caught?" There was a wicked smile on her face, and I had the feeling she might not have been half as pleased with herself if we'd stolen Amanda's box back from anyone other than Heidi Bragg.

"Seriously," I agreed.

She pulled the door open and bright light from the hallway flooded the laundry room, momentarily blinding me.

When I could see again, I found myself staring into the faces of Heidi Bragg and the rest of the I-Girls.

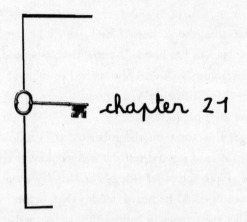

chapter 21

"What were you doing in there?" Heidi's voice was shaking, whether with rage or fear I couldn't tell.

"Probably having seven minutes in heaven!" The dark-haired girl who *hadn't* gotten soda spilled on her stared at me and Callie like we were something nasty she'd discovered on her shoe and was eager to scrape off.

"More like seven minutes in *hell* if it involves either of these two," said Lexa Booker (what, was she now Lexi?!), who was in my bio class and who I hadn't realized was an I-Girl. She was staring daggers at me and Callie.

"I mean it. What were you *doing* in there?" Heidi repeated.

A couple of juniors whose names I didn't know and who I didn't recognize from any of the play rehearsals I'd attended walked past us. "Yo, man," one of them called to a guy down the hall. "What *up*?!" In the distance, I heard the sound of the doorbell ringing.

"Why, Heidi, do you have something in there you don't want us to find?" Callie's voice was strong and sure, her hands in fists on her hips.

The doorbell rang again, and I had the vague sense that someone should answer it as another group of people I didn't remember being in the cast walked by, calling over their shoulders to people behind them to follow.

"You're crazy, you know that?" Heidi shouted at me and Callie. "You're crazy and your friend is crazy and the only reason you think she's so special is because you're *all crazy*!" Heidi's face was grotesque, contorted with rage until she was nearly unrecognizable.

"No, Heidi, actually she *is* special," Callie said. "*You're* the one who's not special."

To my amazement, Callie's insult enraged Heidi so thoroughly she practically convulsed, even though I didn't think it was that terrible a thing to say. I'd heard worse. From Heidi, actually.

"You will so live to regret saying that." Heidi's voice was shaking with rage.

By now the hallway was so crowded Callie and I and Heidi and the I-Girls were slowly being pressed up against opposite walls of the hallway as more and more kids flowed past, oblivious to the drama.

"Who are all these people?" asked the now soggy I-Girl.

But Heidi was still staring bullets at me and Callie. "I want you to tell me what you were doing in that room."

"It's just a laundry room," I said as a group of girls pushing through the crowd jostled Callie and me in the direction of the front door. "You have some embarrassing dirty laundry?"

"Hal Bennett, you are a total—" But the last part of her sentence was lost as Callie and I pushed our way through the crowd and outside into the cold night air.

The scene on the front lawn was total pandemonium. In the time we'd been inside, dozens of cars had parked on the block, and what seemed to be hundreds of people were streaming toward the Braggs'. Most of the faces looked vaguely familiar from the Endeavor hallways, but a couple of the guys were wearing Harrison jackets, from this really artsy-fartsy school across town; I wondered how a party attended by half the population of Endeavor High and half the population of our archrivals was going to end.

You didn't have to be an expert in adolescent behavior to know there was only one answer to that question: not well.

I took Callie by the hand and pulled her down to the corner, glad that Nia had suggested a place to meet that wouldn't be in the middle of what was shaping up to be one of the biggest parties in Orion's history.

To my amazement, when we found Nia, she was still energetically texting.

"What are you *doing*?" I demanded. "Who are you texting?"

Nia looked up and met my confused gaze with a clear, confident one. "Everyone," she answered simply. Then she looked down at her screen, typed something, and added, "Well, I mean, *I'm* not texting everyone." Her face, when she glanced up at me again, was a smirk. "Cisco is."

And suddenly the massive party forming just behind me was a little less mysterious.

"Um, Nia," Callie asked. "What *exactly* are you saying?"

Nia typed one last thing, then slipped her brother's phone into her bag and smiled at us, her face the picture of innocence. "Didn't you get one?"

Callie and I looked at each other, then simultaneously reached for our phones. I had one missed text, and I opened it.

PARTY AT THE BRAGGS', GUYS.
C U THERE! CISCO

"You know what's bad about having a brother who's the most popular guy in the junior class?" Nia asked, and Callie and I both stared at her expectantly.

Nia laughed. "Nothing," she said. "Now wait for me here. I've gotta give my brother his phone back."

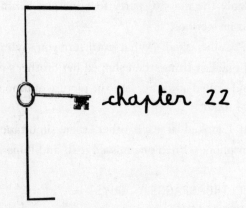 chapter 22

When Nia returned and said, "Follow me," neither of us asked any questions, but after walking in silence for a minute or two, Callie abruptly stopped and I did, too. "Nia, where are we *going* anyway?"

"Your house," Nia said, like it was the most natural thing in the world for us to be headed over to Callie's. "Now, can we please discuss the fact that everything in the Bragg household is *shiny*? Do they, like, spray it with something?"

Standing still, Callie sighed. "Look, I know my dad's not, you know, Father of the Year, but he's going to notice if the three of us march in with *this*"—she indicated the box she'd insisted on carrying—"and, like, ask to borrow his blowtorch to open it."

"He's not home," Nia answered. She hadn't stopped when Callie did, so after exchanging a look, the two of us hustled to catch up to her.

"And how, exactly, do you know that?" Callie asked, just slightly out of breath from our brief jog. We passed the guard in his gatehouse and he gave us a friendly wave. Given everything we'd just discovered, I breathed a sigh of relief that he let us pass instead of, oh, taking out a machine gun and ordering us to lie on the ground until he could summon Chief Bragg.

Nia smiled and waved back at him and the three of us took advantage of the green light to cross Willow Avenue.

"As I was saying, how do you know my dad's not home?" Callie repeated when we were safely on the other side of the street from The Acres, heading south toward Callie's house.

The three of us were walking side by side, and when I glanced over at her, I could see Nia's smile of self-satisfaction. "I got my mom to invite him over for a late dinner with my parents. I knew we'd need a place to spread out with this thing." She indicated the box, then added, "My parents are Colombian. Let's just say they eat dinner late."

"Oh my god, I totally saw them talking to him when we left!" said Callie. I gestured to her that I could take the box, but she said she was okay, and we walked along in silence for a few minutes. I couldn't believe Nia had thought so far ahead. While I'd been worrying about whether we'd even be able to find Amanda's box, Nia had been planning where we'd go to catalog its contents.

As we passed under a streetlight, Nia checked the cool, chunky watch on her wrist. "Cisco's picking up me and Hal at midnight. That gives us a little over an hour."

I nodded. Was there nothing Nia hadn't taken care of?

We walked for several minutes before Callie broke the silence. "Hal, why did you say it was dangerous for us to be together?" Her voice was quiet, but it carried in the still night air.

I took a deep breath. It was time to come clean.

"I need to tell you guys something . . ." I started, and as the suburban neighborhood we were walking through slowly evolved into the countryside nearer Callie's house, I told them about my trip to see Frieda and her warning about Dr. Joy being with *them*. I'd expected the girls to be mad at me for making the trip to see Frieda without telling them, but they just let me talk, not interrupting my story until I got to the part where Frieda said it was dangerous to be together.

"Oh my god!" Callie gasped.

"Yeah," I agreed.

We turned onto Crab Apple Road as I finished the story. It was a cool night, but we were walking fast and I was sweating. I unzipped my jacket.

"Maybe Amanda didn't know it was dangerous for us to be together," Callie suggested. "Maybe we need to take Frieda's warning seriously."

"What?" demanded Nia, her voice sharp. "You're saying we should separate because that Frieda woman said so?"

Callie shook her head. "Not exactly. I just mean . . . that inscription on the watch, wanting us to work together. It totally, like, flies in the face of Frieda's warning. Maybe Amanda didn't know the whole story." We started up Callie's driveway, the light of her front porch like a beacon.

Now it was my turn to object. "I think Amanda *did* know. I'm sure of it. I think she knew we might get spooked and separate and she wanted to make sure that didn't happen." Suddenly, the final piece of the puzzle of Amanda's gift fell into place so surely I could almost hear it, like the click of a key turning in a lock. The realization stopped me dead in my tracks. "That's why she gave me a watch."

Nia and Callie were a few steps ahead of me, on Callie's front porch, and now Nia turned back to where I was still standing in the driveway. "Watch out, you mean?" she suggested.

I was looking at her and Callie but not seeing them. "Yeah. I mean no." I focused my eyes on the girls. "Not watch out for *them*." I thought of Frieda's mysterious *they*. "Watch out for *us*. Watch out for each other."

"Take care of each other," Callie said quietly.

There was a moment of silence as Callie's words sank in, then Nia said, "Um, this is all getting a little kumbaya for me, okay, kids? And we've got work to do." She took the box from Callie, stumbling briefly as she felt its full weight.

"God, Callie, have you been secretly working out or something? This thing is heavy."

"What?" asked Callie, distractedly pushing open the front door that apparently wasn't locked. "Oh, yeah, I guess it is."

Nia and I followed her inside. As I stepped across the threshold, I briefly wondered what the house would be like. Her dad had seemed normal enough tonight, but I'd seen him downtown a few times over the last few months and he'd been in pretty bad shape—unshaven, unshowered, looking like he might have slept in his clothes. Would the house be weird, or look like it used to back when we were friends in sixth grade?

But inside everything looked totally normal. Callie headed into the living room and pointed for Nia to put the box down on the coffee table, then went around turning on the lights. She disappeared through an archway, and I saw a bunch of chairs circling a space where a dining room table should have been but where instead there was just . . . nothing. But when she came back carrying glasses of water and a bag of pretzels, she didn't mention the missing table and so neither did I.

Then, as if on cue, we all took our places on the floor around the low coffee table.

The rich wood glowed in the soft light of Callie's living room, each piece of turquoise shining like a ray of starlight. As I stared at the box, thinking about how no one was ever, ever going to take it away from us again, I felt as if a massive weight had been lifted from my shoulders.

"We've still got to open it, you know?" Nia pointed out.

"You said something about buttons?" I prompted Callie.

She nodded. "You can't exactly *see* them," she explained, then closed her eyes, feeling across the surface of the box briefly. "Here." Her eyes flew open. "This is one." She took Nia's hand and placed it where hers had been, and as soon as Nia said, "Yes, I feel it!" she took my index finger and used it to push Nia's finger aside and show me what they'd both felt.

At first, I didn't know what Callie and Nia were talking about, but then I did. The button was so small, and it fit into the pattern so naturally, that when I accidentally moved my finger off it, I had trouble finding it again. All three of us rose to our knees and leaned forward, our faces so close to the box that our heads knocked gently together. At first, it was impossible to see with our eyes what we'd felt with our fingers, but then Nia exclaimed, "It's an eye!"

"What?"

She tilted the box slightly to catch the light and show us what she meant. "See? This is some kind of . . . it's a lizard, I think."

Her word choice reminded me of something, and as she traced the outline of the creature with her finger, I suddenly realized what it was. "The car!" I shouted. "The drawings on the car."

Digging frantically in my pocket for my phone, I yanked it out, then shuffled through the photos until I came to the ones we'd taken of Thornhill's car before we washed it. "Look!" I said, when I'd hit on the one I wanted. I turned the screen toward Callie and Nia.

"Oh my god," Nia murmured.

The lizard she was touching on the box was an exact replica of the one Amanda had drawn on the car.

Or, the one on the car had been a replica of the one on the box.

"Push the button," said Callie.

Nia did. We all waited a minute, but nothing happened.

Callie exhaled and I realized I, too, had been holding my breath.

"Wait a minute," I said. "If there's a lizard, there might be the other animals, too." I pointed around at each of the girls as I spoke her totem. "Bear. Night owl." Pointing at myself, I said, "Cougar."

"Coyote," Nia said, adding Amanda's totem.

"Coyote," I repeated.

"Okay," said Callie. "Let's find them."

It was the definition of looking for a needle in a haystack. Fine, nearly invisible lines crissed and crossed, turning into leaves and elaborate abstract designs just as they seemed about to reveal themselves to be one of our totem animals. At first we were reluctant to mark the box, but when we found the cougar and immediately lost it, we agreed to use Nia's lipstick to mark with a slightly sticky X each button when we found it.

It felt like we'd been sitting for hours when, finally, the floor lamp Callie had brought over to the table illuminated the final totem: the night owl. I felt like howling at the sky as if I were an actual cougar, and I might have done it, too, if Nia's next comment hadn't brought me crashing down to earth.

"What do we do now that we have them?"

I raised my eyes to meet Callie's and Nia's stares. We'd come so far. Surely there *had* to be an Oz at the end of this yellow brick road.

"And, guys, do you think that's somebody's totem?" Nia asked, pointing to the lizard.

Callie looked puzzled. "Well, whose?"

Nia executed her trademark eye roll. "Obviously, I don't know whose. But there are our totems, and Amanda's. So I am just making the leap."

I broke in. "Cut it out. Who knows whose it is? Maybe it is someone she looked for and never found. But it probably is significant because it was on the car."

Callie snapped her fingers. "The car. It could be the person who helped her graffiti the car!"

"And who is he?" I groaned.

"Or *she*," Nia countered.

"Whatev. However you slice it, the lizard is important," I agreed.

Her voice utterly confident, Callie decided. "We push the buttons. All five of them."

Nia shrugged slightly. "Didn't do anything before."

"We only pushed one before," Callie pointed out.

"One, five, what's the difference?" asked Nia. "What does it matter if we push them all at once or one at a time?"

Callie stared at me, then at Nia. "Come together," she said. "That was the message. Come together."

With that, she put two fingers on the box, one on each of the totem's eyes nearest her. Without speaking, Nia did the same. I found the button of the last remaining totem.

"On my count," Callie said. "One. Two. Three."

I pressed my finger against the button as hard as I possibly could, but the force I exerted was unnecessary. No sooner had I put the slightest pressure on the eye of the coyote than I felt something deep inside the box fall into place.

There was an almost inaudible click, and then a spring-loaded drawer in the box flew open.

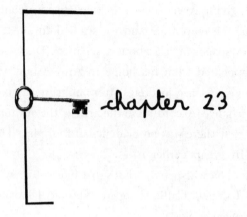

chapter 23

Nia gasped. I could feel my hands shaking. For a second we were all too shocked to move, and then Nia slipped her hand into the drawer. There must have been over a hundred pieces of paper stuffed into it—she couldn't get them all at once and had to take out a bunch, then reach back in and get more.

"What is it?" Callie asked eagerly. "Let me see!"

"Chill," Nia said sharply. There were still papers left in the drawer, but Callie and I ignored them and huddled around Nia to look at what she was holding.

"It's a map," I said. The paper Nia was holding was an ordinary road map; there are a dozen like it in my mom's car. I let my eyes follow a thick black line until they came to . . . "It's Maryland," I said. Sure enough, when Nia unfolded the map, it was a Rand McNally guide to Virginia and Maryland. We examined every square inch, but except for what looked like a coffee stain in one corner, there were no marks anywhere on it.

"Okay, okay, let's just . . . just look at something else," Callie said, giving voice to the impatience we were all feeling.

Nia put the map aside and we studied the next piece of paper, a newspaper article about a scientist, Dr. Cole Tobias, who'd disappeared from his home in Ann Arbor, Michigan, without leaving a trace, just days after publishing a major paper on climate change. According to the article, the authorities had concluded that there was no evidence of foul play. The article was dated five years earlier.

"Callie," Nia whispered, "that's just like your . . ."

"Yeah, I know," Callie snapped. Nia and I looked at her, and she shrugged. "Sorry."

"Does the name Cole Tobias, age"—Nia glanced at the paper—"forty-five, mean anything to you?"

Callie and I shook our heads and Nia put the clipping on top of the map. "Okay, strike two."

We all read the next page, a review of a book called *Mapping the Human Genome* by a woman named Maude Cooper.

"Wait a minute," I said. Maude Cooper. Maude Cooper. Where had I seen that name before?

"Thornhill's computer!" I snapped my fingers.

"What?" Nia asked, jerking her head up.

Suddenly I realized that I had not told them about when Cornelia hacked into Thornhill's computer and that I got to take a longer look at the list of names until someone shut us down. I caught them up on everything I'd seen as quickly as I could.

"Amanda and Beatrice Rossiter were *friends*?" Nia's and Callie's faces wore expressions of the purest shock.

I nodded. "I know. It's crazy."

"And you're *sure* you saw the name Maude Cooper on that list?" Nia asked.

"Positive," I said.

Nia stared bullets at me. "Any other earth-shattering developments or secrets you'd like to share at the eleventh hour, Hal Bennett?"

"I think that about covers it."

Nia shook her head at my attempt at understatement, then studied the pile on the table. "We need some space to put the things in this box that are significant."

"But *everything's* significant." Callie's voice was frustrated. "Just because some of it seems insignificant to *us* doesn't mean it's not important."

Nia opened her mouth, and from the expression on her face, I knew she was about to bite Callie's head off. "Let's create a separate pile of stuff we *understand* the significance of," I said quickly.

"Oh, you understand the significance of *this*?" Nia waved the article about Maude Cooper's book.

"Better than I understand the significance of *that*." I pointed at the map of Maryland on the coffee table.

Nia looked down at the pile of papers on her lap, then glanced at her watch and groaned. "We can't spend ten minutes on every piece of paper or Cisco will be here before we get through a tenth of this." She took a bunch of papers off the top of the pile on her lap and handed them to Callie. She handed another stack to me. Without moving from our uncomfortable positions on the floor, we all started reading.

On the top of my pile was another map—this one of greater Los Angeles. Again, there was no writing on it anywhere, and I put it on top of the article about Dr. Cole Tobias and the Maryland map—the Mysterious but Probably Really Important pile. The next piece of paper was another newspaper clipping, this one of an obituary. A man named George Chang had fallen to his death while hiking the Appalachian Trail. I skimmed the article. Mr. Chang had been an early investor in Silicon Valley, his own start-up, blah blah blah. Nothing in the article made any sense to me, and I put it on the mystery pile.

"Callie, look!" Nia read aloud from the piece of paper on top of her pile. "Orion's Dr. Ursula Leary was honored by the National Institute of Science for her work on locating the galaxy Alpha Benton-554." Callie was leaning over Nia's shoulder and reading with her. "It's from the *Orion Herald*," Nia explained to me, eyes still on the paper. "And it's circled." I crawled over to where they were sitting. The article had a picture of Callie's mom, and it explained how she'd been honored at a luncheon in Washington, D.C. There was part of another article on the page, too, something about funding for a local animal shelter. But part of it was ripped off, and the bright red circle around the article about Callie's mom made it clear Amanda hadn't saved the piece of paper because of her interest in the good work being done by our local ASPCA.

"My mom got this award *two years* before Amanda came

here." Callie looked up and our eyes met. "Why would Amanda have this?"

"Yeah, and it's the *actual* newspaper, not a computer print-out." Nia touched the newsprint lightly.

"She was reading the *Orion Herald* two years before she came to Orion?" Callie asked, incredulous.

"Apparently," Nia said, placing the article on top of the clipping about Maude Cooper.

I looked down at the top piece of paper on my lap. In my confusion, it took me a minute to focus on the words, but when I did, I saw it was an official-looking document with the words Medical Examiner's Office printed in thick black type at the top. It was a death certificate for Annie Beckendorf.

"Wait a minute, that's the woman in the article, the one who was killed in the car crash!" I said to myself out loud.

"What are you talking about?" Nia and Callie asked together.

"Um, yet another detail I forgot to mention," I offered, wrinkling my face with guilt.

"Hal!" Nia yelled, and Callie punched me in the arm.

Hard.

"Hey, *who* wasn't talking to *whom*?" I reminded them, matching their irritation with my own. "Anyway, I didn't *know* it might be significant. How many hundreds of posts to the website do we get every *day*? You guys could have read it there yourselves, anyway!" I rubbed my arm where Callie's fist had slammed into it and told them about the article that had been sent into the website describing the woman who'd died in the car accident in California.

"California," Callie mused. "Those movie tickets were from California."

I pointed at the pile of mysteries. "There's also a map of L.A. there."

"Guys," said Nia, eyes on the paper on her lap, "listen."

Nia started reading aloud, but the document was so thick with legalese it took me a minute to translate what she was saying. ". . . does herewith become the legal guardian of her younger sister, a minor. Robin Beckendorf's legal rights extend (but are not limited) to choosing an appropriate school for said minor; using funds from the accounts provided by their mother, the deceased Annie Beckendorf (hereinafter referred to simply as "Annie") for any and all expenses deemed necessary by Robin; signing any necessary legal forms relating to said schooling or expenses—"

Callie interrupted. "I don't get it. Who are these people?"

"Beckendorf," Nia said. "That's the last name of the woman who died in the car crash and her daughters."

"Do you think they're friends of Amanda's?" I asked. "Or relatives?" I'd gotten so used to the idea of Amanda traveling solo it was weird to insert a bunch of cousins where before there had been no one.

Nia and Callie shrugged. "Anything's possible," said Callie. She looked back down at the papers in front of her, and there was silence for a moment as we all started reading again. To my amazement, the very next piece of paper on my lap was an envelope addressed to Max and Annie Beckendorf, 451 Lilac

Drive, Denver, CO, 56783. There was no return address. Inside the envelope was a card with a stork carrying a pink blanket with a baby in it. I opened the card.

> Dearest Annie and Max,
> Congratulations on the arrival
> of your little one. She chose her parents wisely.
> All best, John Joy

I gasped. "Dr. Joy!" I shouted. "Dr. Joy wrote this Annie Beckendorf woman a card when her baby was born."

I passed the card to Nia and Callie, but after they'd both read it, none of us had any idea what the note meant. I put it on top of the significant pile and went back to looking at the papers on my lap.

I had no clue what to make of a form letter dated September fifth of this school year, signed by Mr. Thornhill and addressed to the parents of Endeavor students. The first page was a schedule of home and away games, and the second was a printout of the statement about the school's zero tolerance on drinking at school-related events whether or not they took place on school grounds. At the bottom of the page, in handwriting that was definitely Amanda's, was the word,

MAYBE?

Maybe *what*? Why had she saved this particular letter from Thornhill, written over a month before she even came to Orion? How had she even *gotten* it, since as far as I knew, she wasn't living in Orion when the letter was sent. Had someone showed it to her once she moved here? Was she planning to use it in a future article in the *Spirit*?

Before I could voice my confusion, Callie shouted, "Hey, look at this!"

She gestured for us to come over to where she was sitting, and I found myself looking at a photo of Amanda at the age of eleven or twelve standing next to an older girl whose face was hard to see under the brim of the baseball cap she was wearing. Amanda looked more regular than I'd ever seen her—no strange costume or hairstyle, no weird accessories. She wore a pair of jean shorts and a red T-shirt with something I couldn't read written on it, looking like a totally average twelve-year-old. Next to the two girls stood a woman who was shading her eyes against the sun as she gazed down at them.

Suddenly I thought of how my mom keeps track of everything on all our family photos. "Flip it over. Maybe it says something on the back."

Nia did. There, on the back of the picture, it said: *The Beckendorf Girls.*

"But . . ." Callie turned the picture over and looked at the threesome again. No doubt about it, the girl in the middle was *definitely* Amanda. Which meant . . .

"Oh my god," Nia breathed. She looked up at me. "Hal, you were right."

"Amanda Valentino is this Beckendorf girl," Callie whispered.

"Her mom, Annie, died in that car crash," Nia added.

"Which means . . ." My heart pounding, I thought back to the paper Nia had read from earlier. "She's got a sister named Robin."

"Who's her guardian," Nia finished.

"But what about her dad?" I asked. "What about . . ." I remembered Dr. Joy's card. "Max Beckendorf?"

"Do you think he's dead, too?" asked Callie.

"Or missing?" offered Nia.

Nia and Callie and I looked at one another, but none of us knew the answer.

Nia dropped her eyes and picked up the next item on her lap. It was a small card that said AMANDA in bright red letters. Underneath the name, in smaller type, the card read: SHE WHO MUST BE LOVED. Nia flipped over the card. The back was blank except for a small line of print that said THE WHATSYOURNAMEMEAN COMPANY.

"She made up her name," Nia said quietly, holding the card. "She picked it because of what it means. Nothing she told us was true." Her voice was sharp as she tossed the card onto the table, where it slid along the glass surface almost to the edge. "Not a word."

"Yes it was," I said.

Nia turned to me, her face awash in the deep betrayal she was feeling. "Her mother is *dead*, Hal, not traveling in Africa or dealing with a divorce. Dead. It was a lie. All of it. Even her name." She pushed angrily at the papers on her lap as if just touching them was enough to sully her.

I put my hand on Nia's arm. Callie didn't say anything, but when I looked over at her, I could see the pain on her face, too.

"She brought us together, and that wasn't a lie," I said. "That's real. And it's more important than whether her name's Hayes or Stone or Valentino or who *cares* what." I realized I was squeezing Nia's arm too hard—as if I was going to force her to believe me. I let go.

There was a pause as I contemplated the stupidity of defending this crazy, lying girl I'd thought we all loved.

And then Callie said, "She's in trouble. Serious trouble. That's not a lie, either."

Nia was silent for what seemed like a long, long time. Finally, she, too, spoke. "Something really, really big is going on. Really big and really bad."

I thought of the doctor at the hospital, the names on Thornhill's list. "And somehow it involves us."

When Nia spoke again, I knew she didn't care anymore that Amanda had lied about her mother or her name. "We have to post this stuff on the site. Maybe whoever sent you the article about her mom knows more."

"Yeah, and maybe they're looking for her, too," Callie said, adding, "Looking in a bad way."

"Yeah, a Bragg way," said Nia with a shudder.

"We'll figure out what we can post. We can do that." I hoped I sounded more confident than I felt. How could we find Amanda before the other people who were looking for her?

They had the chief of police on their side. Doctors. Hospital guards. All the adults I'd been taught to think I could rely on and trust—they were all working for whatever dark, evil people were hunting Amanda.

This was impossible.

No sooner had the horror of what we were up against hit me than I felt Callie's fingers slip into mine. "We have Amanda," she said quietly. "They may have a lot on their side, but we have her. We have her, and we have each other."

Into the silence of Callie's words, a car horn beeped twice. Cisco.

Callie squeezed my hand and I squeezed hers. A second later, I felt Nia press her shoulder into mine.

"Come together," she said.

"Right now," added Callie.

"Over me," I finished.

And even though we knew Cisco was waiting for us outside, for a long moment we just sat there in the silence, leaning on one another.

A BIG ROUND OF THANKS

You guys should have seen the fireworks when Nia saw my first version of the story. "Finished?! What do you mean, you're finished? Where's your list of references?" I looked at her like she was crazy—it's not like I had written a research paper. Still, as she none-too-gently reminded me, I have to give credit where credit is due. Especially since we couldn't have gotten this far without everybody at The Amanda Project posting leads, discussing clues, and making sure we never, ever give up. It's you guys we have to thank for helping us solve the mystery of the secret room at Endeavor (http://www.theamandaproject.com/clues/the-key-to-the-secret-room), which clued us in to the possibility of a secret room at the Braggs' house, which was where we found Amanda's box, which had all that stuff about her family, which . . . you get the picture.

Bottom line is, even though we could only do a tiny number of individual shout-outs, we want all of you to know how impressed we are with the community you've helped us build on TheAmandaProject.com.

MANY THANKS TO:

Dem_94 (page 18)

Cecile Reeve (page 18)

Gracie Hayes (page 18, page 220)

urban_hippie (page 28)

Rachiebaby (hot pink raincoat, page 35)

AwesomeAnna93 (Mr. V's art class, page 62, page 156)

ChelleAtwood (page 74)

Emily.K (E. Knight, page 74)

PoppyGloom (L. Feltz, page 74, page 99)

Mrs. Hayworth (page 90)

Wispofacloud (Ms. Wisp, page 91)

Samthy (page 99)

Soccerfanatic (Amanda Valentory, page 99)

The Midnighter (page 102)

NightmareGirl (Samara Cole, page 143)

Sol Rosa (page 146)

Stef_Stone (page 147)

Luvlcx3 (Laden Chapel, page 147)

Theresaax2 (page 179)

ArtsyFartsy (page 200)

Willow (page 203)

Gemma Stone (page 220)

FASCINATING STORIES AND ARTWORK ABOUT
AMANDA CONTINUE TO FLOOD IN FROM ALL OVER.
HERE ARE TWO TOTALLY AMAZING PIECES! PLEASE
KEEP THEM COMING, AND CHECK OUT THOUSANDS
MORE AT WWW.THEAMANDAPROJECT.COM!

–HAL, CALLIE, AND NIA

AMANDA POEM

A trickster in a place that behaves

Once you meet her things are never the same

You blink your eyes and she's there

You blink your eyes, you see her hair

But it is only a trick of the light

The coyote, after all, is more than bright

So follow the clues

Decide the don'ts and the dos

And after the answers become clear

You find out all along she was here

About the Author: Rowan Knight is a thirteen-year-old from the U.K.
She loves to daydream and to play her trumpet, but she hates
mushrooms with a passion. She one day hopes to be a surgeon so
she can save someone's life.

Character Screen Name: SquankyDonkey
Member Since: March 24, 2010
**She believes Amanda is telling the truth, and finds the need to clean her
room before she does her homework.**

MYSTERIOUS AMANDA

About the Artist: Alex Immerman, fifteen, resides in the Twin Cities of Minnesota. She loves art and writing and aspires to become a published author in the future.

Character Screen Name: AlexInvisible
Member Since: May 19, 2010
She sometimes pretends to have a British accent, is completely indifferent to tuna salad, and believes Amanda is "uNiQuE."

shattered . . .

Once upon a time, there was a girl named Amanda, the physical and emotional equivalent of a glass of sparkling champagne. And one day, Amanda dropped into Nia's life, jumbled it around, shimmered it up, and forced her to look at life from a totally new perspective. Then Amanda disappeared without a word.

And Nia's fairy tale turned into a nightmare.

Hello, faithful readers, Nia here. It's finally my turn to take over. Not that I don't trust Hal and Callie's accounts, but we all know who's the most on top of things around here. I thought I would start off with the above. Because it explains exactly what Amanda did. She took my life, upended it, and vanished. To be fair, she did leave me with friends I never expected to have and, well, a ME I never expected to be, but that is all in the story. *Shattered*. Look for it.

What happens next? I can't tell you too much more, but the contents of Amanda's box definitely hold the key to her past. And after our most recent encounters with the menacing, shadowy people chasing her, I can see why she's gone underground. But fear not. There is no lead we won't run down. And that, my friends, gets us closer to Amanda every day.

Until then, keep sleuthing, and see you on the site.

—Nia

Peter Silsbee has published five young adult novels, including *The Big Way Out* and *Love Among the Hiccups*. Peter also has a band, The Haywood Brothers. He lives with his wife and family in Brooklyn.

This is the story of Amanda Valentino. She makes things happen for her own reasons.

CORNELIA'S CODE

Hey, Guys!

Cornelia here. Have you ever seen someone and wondered if they know what you know? Or wondered how to let them know that you know that they know what you know, without actually saying it, just in case they don't know what you know? Luckily, I've come up with the perfect solution—data-matrix codes! They're BIG in Japan, which means they're headed this way. (Um, Pokémon? Sushi? Hello Kitty? Need I say more?)

I looove using new technology (duh), which is why I am SO excited for you guys to start using the codes to help Hal, Callie, and Nia find Amanda.

Basically, a datamatrix code is a bar code like the ones you're used to seeing in stores . . . only way cooler. You don't need a special scanner, just a phone with camera and internet connection. To read them, all you have to do is:

- Use your phone to download the 2D Bar Code reader software at http://theamandaproject.mobi/thereader
- Fire it up (it's usually under Applications)
- Snap a picture of the code using your phone's camera

And voilà! The browser on your phone will automatically unlock the magic programmed into the code—a secret website with video, messages, pictures, and more!

So, what's the secret in this code? You'll have to scan to find out. And remember— the next time you see a code it might be a message from me, or from Amanda, or from that new girl at school who wants to know if you know what she knows . . .

Over and out
— Cornelia B.